GUARDING HIS CHILD

KAREN KIRST

LOVE INSPIRED SUSPENSE
INSPIRATIONAL ROMANCE

LOVE INSPIRED® SUSPENSE
INSPIRATIONAL ROMANCE

Recycling programs for this product may not exist in your area.

ISBN-13: 978-1-335-58757-2

Guarding His Child

Love Inspired
22 Adelaide St. West, 41st Floor
Toronto, Ontario M5H 4E3, Canada
www.LoveInspired.com

Printed in U.S.A.

He shall not be afraid of evil tidings: his heart is fixed,
trusting in the Lord.
—*Psalms* 112:7

To Brianne Griggs. You inspire me.

ONE

Deputy Skye Saddler stared in disbelief at the eviction notice taped to her door. The southern Mississippi heat was no match for the shame licking her insides. Lewis had followed through with his threat to kick her out of the apartment complex. He'd gotten tired of the late payments and excuses, and she couldn't fault him for it. The landlord had given her more chances than she'd deserved.

Her radio crackled, and the dispatcher relayed a report of a possible crime in progress. Ripping the slip off the door, she jumped into her cruiser and advised the call center that she was responding. She hurtled along the country roads toward the designated address, a rental house that had been vacant for at least a decade. Teenagers could've chosen to use it as a hangout. Or a squatter could've moved in.

The word *squatter* made her thoughts circle back to her own predicament. The news that she was homeless wouldn't stay contained for long. Her reputation would take another serious hit. Some would say the apple didn't fall far from the tree, insinuating she wasn't that different from her late mother.

Skye could handle their whispers and bless-your-hearts. What worried her was Sheriff Hines's reaction. Her inability to pay her bills would reflect poorly on the department, and the sheriff always had his eye on the next election.

She passed farms, mobile homes, a broiler chicken outfit and a struggling gas station. Dusk filtered through the magnolias, picking up the cracks in the neglected stretch of road. Wind gusts batted the cruiser. Fat clouds hovered above the lush fields. Raindrops splattered her windshield. Through the encroaching gloom, she spotted the house and a single vehicle in the driveway—a two-door coupe that had seen better days. She slowed, made the turn and parked beside it, noting both windows were partially rolled down.

Up close, the house's state of disrepair was jarring. The clapboard siding was dingy and chipped. Trees clustered against one side, shading the moss-coated roof shingles. The left and rear sides were exposed to the elements, with not even a single bush to protect from the wind and rain.

She popped her door handle. "Dispatch, who called this in?"

"An unidentified female. She heard a scream from inside the residence. She ended the call before I could ask her name or advise her to stay put."

"Copy that."

Did the vehicle belong to the caller, or had she been too frightened to stick around and fled the scene?

Skye unholstered her Glock 19 and, carefully making her way onto the porch, nudged the open door with her shoe. "Police department. Anyone here?"

The smell of mildew filled her nostrils. Dust coated furniture that was straight out of a time capsule. A dead mouse lay in the fireplace, and soda cans were stacked on a windowsill.

Skye heard a gurgling sound, and her pulse tripped over itself. She continued past the couch and smothered a gasp. A young brunette lay on her back in a pool of blood. The stab wounds were too numerous to count.

"Help."

The gossamer-soft plea spurred Skye to act. She used her radio to request medical assistance and snagged the small blanket draped over the couch. Kneeling beside the victim, she tried to stanch the flow from the more serious wounds.

"Ambulance is on its way, ma'am." She studied the features streaked with blood and dust and thought she looked familiar.

"Baby." Her lips barely moved. "Nash's baby."

Nash Wilder of Wilder Ranch? The man who made Skye feel like she'd fallen into a patch of poison oak?

The victim's lids fluttered open, revealing hazel eyes. Skye sat back on her haunches.

"Lucy?"

There was no denying the woman clinging to life was her best friend from school—Lucy Ackerman. She'd dyed her light hair a darker brown and grown it out, and she'd put on enough weight to look healthy, for a change. An addiction to drugs had all but severed Lucy's relationship with her family and friends, and she'd moved away from Tulip years ago.

"Lucy? It's Skye." She rested her trembling hand on her shoulder. "Hang on a while longer, okay? Can you do that for me?"

She stared at Skye. "Eden." She struggled to speak. "Nash's daughter."

Skye glanced around, belatedly noticing a sippy cup on the kitchen counter. The blanket she'd pressed to Lucy's chest was pink with baby ducks. Her stomach churned. Was there an infant in the house? Had she been harmed?

Leaving Lucy was difficult since these could be her last moments on earth, but Skye had no choice.

Weapon in one hand, she cleared a bathroom and bedroom. The kitchen didn't hold clues other than the sippy cup. The second bedroom was vacant. The third's door was shut. Perspiring now, she turned the knob and eased into the room, praying for the first time since the car accident that had ended life as she'd known it.

A bare, dirty mattress rested on a metal frame. Her breath whooshed out. Where was the child?

She skirted the footboard and peered in the space between the bed and the wall. A crash sounded behind her and her muscles tensed. Before she could react, a body slammed into her, propelling her into the window. Her forehead slammed against the dirty, cracked glass, splintering it further. Shards pierced her skin, pain exploding through her head as blood trickled into her eyes.

The door scraped shut. Skye gained her footing and swayed, catching herself with a palm against the wall. She heard the back door opening and closing, and she pushed upright, gritting her teeth against the sudden intense headache.

Advising Dispatch of the situation, she pursued the intruder outside just as the skies opened up. Pounding rain hampered her vision. Through the trees, she caught sight of a black-clad figure. She gave chase, but the rain and her injury slowed her down. Within minutes, she'd lost sight of him. Thoughts of Lucy's devastating injuries and the undetermined location of the child sent her back to the house.

She called Deputy Hank Flowers and asked him to head directly to Nash Wilder's house. If his whereabouts these past few hours couldn't be accounted for, he would become her first suspect.

Distant sirens heralded the ambulance's approach. She jogged around the house to the driveway, only to stop short and cock her head. Was that a child's cry?

Wiping the rain and blood from her face, she hurried to the driver's side of the two-door coupe. The front seats were empty, as were the footwells. She bent closer for a better look at the cramped rear area and was shocked to see a small toddler huddled beneath a blanket. She was clinging to a stuffed animal, her straight blond hair framing her pink cheeks.

Skye pulled the door open and sprang the seat forward. The girl's electric blue eyes—exactly like Nash Wilder's—peered up at Skye in panic. Tears welled and spilled over.

Crouching, she reached out and touched the child's foot. "My name's Skye. I'm here to help you."

When she didn't respond, Skye gently scooped her up and carried her beneath the porch awning. She needed to check on Lucy, but the toddler didn't need to see the violent scene inside.

Was she truly Lucy and Nash's child? The pair had dated their junior and senior years of high school, but that was over a decade ago. Skye hadn't approved of the way Nash had treated her friend, and she'd let him know it on several occasions. She'd been relieved when he'd joined the Marines right after graduation. Lucy, on the other hand, hadn't taken it well. Her occasional drug use had become a serious problem, and her mom, Maeve, had eventually kicked her out. Lucy had left Tulip for good. Skye had only seen her sporadically in the last few years.

The girl continued to cry pitifully, and Skye gazed down at her.

"Eden, I'm going to help you."

Although she likely didn't understand, she seemed to calm.

The ambulance wheeled into the drive. The paramedics emerged with their gear, and she urged them to check on Lucy first. Her own cuts could wait, and Eden didn't appear to have any injuries.

Another cruiser pulled up, and Skye's jaw tightened as Sergeant Lee Chen emerged. He strode through the rain to join her on the porch, his sharp, glittering gaze assessing them.

"What happened?"

She laid out the timeline and relayed Lucy's claim about Nash.

Chen's brows edged up. "How Wilder manages to keep his private life private in this town, I'll never know."

Skye knew the answer to that but kept it to herself. Nash had perfected the art of deflection. His face was in the dictionary under the word *evasive*. Had Nash and Lucy agreed to keep their daughter hidden from the people of Tulip?

Nash had returned from his long stint in the Marines four years ago. He must have had the opportunity to strike up a renewed romance with his former love. Could he have pressured Lucy to stay away from their hometown? Maybe he was embarrassed to acknowledge the relationship because of her lifestyle choices. He was serious about continuing the Wilder legacy in the wake of his father's death. Maybe he hadn't wanted anything to soil his reputation.

Her phone buzzed. "It's Hank."

Their conversation was brief. When she ended it, Chen filled in the blanks.

"Wilder has an alibi?"

"Hank located Nash and his ranch hands in the back

pasture. They were on horseback and working cattle. He couldn't have made it from here to the ranch in the time it took for Hank to arrive. Plus, he and his hands say they haven't left the property all day."

One of the paramedics emerged and met Skye's gaze. He shook his head, and her heart sank through the soles of her shoes and into the Mississippi mud. She closed her eyes and inhaled Eden's sweet baby smell.

We'll find out who did this to you, Lucy, and bring them to justice.

"As soon as you've both been checked out, take her on over to the ranch." Chen's voice held no sympathy. He was a transplant from Jackson and didn't know Lucy. "Interview Wilder. Maybe he can tell us what the victim was doing here and who would want her dead."

"And after that? I can't leave Eden with Nash until his paternity is verified."

"You're certified for kinship and respite care through CPS. She's your responsibility until this is sorted out."

Skye swallowed her protest. Both Chen and Hank were also certified by the Mississippi Department of Child Protection Services. Either one could assume responsibility for Eden. If she argued the point, however, Chen would want to know why. He obviously hadn't yet heard about her eviction. She'd like to duck that conversation for as long as possible.

The paramedics treated her cuts and covered them with a bandage. They checked Eden and didn't find any cause for concern. After transferring the car seat and diaper bag from Lucy's car to her cruiser, Skye headed for the ranch.

Nash's place was located on the far side of town. Skye skirted the historic downtown area and continued five miles west. She passed the bowling alley, boat manufacturing plant and the Piggly Wiggly. Her fingernails dug into the wheel as she drove beneath the arch advertising Wilder Ranch in stark black letters. She hadn't been on Wilder land since before Nash's father, Wes, died more than four years ago.

A painted wooden sign directed visitors to the ranch's farm stand, advertising fresh vegetables and assorted homemade goods. She continued driving along the lane past a serene pond framed by old oaks and magnolia trees. The road curved to the left between fenced-off pastures, several barns, a greenhouse and garden. The ranch house had new white board-and-batten siding, and the shutters were painted a dark brown to match the wood posts. The property was flourishing under Nash's supervision. He obviously cared about his ranch's legacy.

She glanced in the rearview mirror. What about his daughter? The fact that the child was unknown in Tulip suggested he likely cared about Eden about as much as he'd cared about Lucy.

Feeling distinctly ungenerous, she parked the cruiser close to the house. The rain had stopped, leaving behind a mist that thickened the encroaching dusk. Beyond the fence, four men on horseback mingled with a herd of cattle and a pair of muddy dogs. One cow didn't seem to want to go along with their plan. A man on a palomino chased after it. His rope sailed through the air and landed around the cow's neck. Nash had practically been born in the saddle, and more than a decade away from the cowboy life hadn't dulled his skills.

A ranch hand joined him, roping the animal's hind legs. Both wore caramel-colored rain slickers splattered with mud. They hadn't noticed her yet.

Skye emerged from the vehicle and retrieved Eden. The toddler's tears had dried, but she looked wary.

"I don't blame you, kid," she murmured.

Hefting Eden onto her hip, Skye walked over to the fence and called out to Nash. His head whipped up, and the other three riders looked, too. He tossed his rope to another cowboy and rode over.

Beneath the shade of his Stetson, his tan, rugged features wore a mix of impatience and curiosity. His vivid blue eyes revealed nothing. Not a spark of fatherly affection. Not a question of why his daughter was in the company of a law enforcement officer. Not even recognition.

Was he really that adept at hiding his thoughts?

"More vague questions, Deputy? Must be something important for me to get two visits from Tulip's finest in one day."

"We need to talk."

His mouth compressed into a thin line. He shifted in the saddle and his horse's tail swished, stirring flies in the humid air. One hand rested on the saddle horn, the other on his thigh. His slicker was unbuttoned, and she saw a tiny rip in his blue-and-white shirt and a smear of mud on his jeans.

"Can it wait? I'm in the middle of something."

"Lucy's dead, Nash. Murdered."

His head reared back. "Lucy Ackerman?"

"Do you know another Lucy?" she retorted. "She was stabbed to death in a vacant house on the far side of town. The point of Hank's visit was to ascertain your whereabouts at the time of the murder. The point of mine is to get your help narrowing down suspects. And, more importantly, to bring your daughter to you." She stared into Eden's round, innocent face. The girl clutched her stuffed bear, her big blue eyes worriedly taking everything in.

"Whoa." He swung one leg over the horse to dismount. "You've got the wrong man. I've never set eyes on that child before today, and I haven't spoken to or heard from Lucy in years."

"That's a conundrum, because Lucy's last wish was for me to reunite Eden with her father. *You.*"

Skye Saddler's presence on his property was as rare as a polar bear sighting on a cattle ranch. The prickly deputy had steered clear of him since his return to Tulip. He wasn't complaining. Skye had always treated him like an unruly yearling.

The starched olive green uniform shirt, shiny badge and firearm added weight to her disdainful stare, and he was reminded she had the authority to make his life miserable. If he didn't hear her out, he could be facing countless speed traps and nuisance fines in his future. Not to mention the rumors that would circulate if she told anyone else this story that he had a child with Lucy.

A sultry breeze tugged at her hair. When on duty, she tamed the espresso-colored curls into some sort of braided knot at the base of her neck. She was a striking woman with her brown skin, arresting green eyes and bow-shaped lips. All the guys in their senior class had been infatuated with her. Most hadn't asked her out because she was a handful. "Sassy," his grandpa would've said.

She cocked her head, her manicured brows arching above her eyes, pulling at the stark-white bandage on her forehead.

"Nash, did you hear what I said?"

He'd heard, all right. He didn't want to believe Lucy was dead. Somewhere in the vicinity of where his heart was supposed to be, he felt hollow. The girl he'd dated way back in high school had been kind and naive. She'd had an infectious laugh, a boundless imagination and eagerness for new experiences. She'd also been emotionally fragile and high-strung. His teenage self hadn't known how to handle the drama, especially as he'd been dealing with his own troubles at home.

After looping Rico's reins around the top rung of the fence, he climbed over and dropped down on her side.

"We both know Lucy's an addict," he said, propping his hands on his hips, "and that's the reason she's avoided Tulip and her mother all these years."

"She wasn't on anything today," Skye snapped, one hand resting protectively on the toddler's back. "Look at her. Can you deny the resemblance?"

Nash took stock of the fine blond hair and elfin face. He looked fully into the child's eyes for the first time and experienced a jolt. It was like looking in the mirror. No doubt about it...she had Wilder eyes.

Skye noticed and leaned in. "You see it, don't you?"

He didn't *want* to see it.

"Is it out of the range of possibility?" she persisted.

"How old is she?" His voice sounded far away to his own ears.

"Around two, I'd guess."

Nash's throat began to close. Almost three years ago, Lucy had come to the ranch. She'd been sober but distraught. For what reason, he couldn't remember now. He'd been dealing with his own roller-coaster emotions, coming home after more than a decade away and trying to cope with his father's death. One thing had led to another, and he'd made a regrettable choice. The next morning, he'd woken to find Lucy had bailed, and he hadn't seen or heard from her again.

Surely, if she'd turned up pregnant, she would've come to him. Lucy wouldn't have kept his own child from him, would she?

TWO

Nash stared at Eden as if she were a ticking time bomb.

"Is there somewhere we can talk?" Skye prompted.

"In the house. Door's unlocked. I'll let the guys know where I'll be and return Rico to the barn."

He climbed back over the fence, hauled his solid, muscular body into the saddle and rode away.

When Skye had awoken that morning, she'd expected it to be a typical spring day where she might have to deal with a domestic dispute, dole out speeding tickets in the school zone or admonish a teenager for swiping a pack of gum. That was classic small-town life. The pace was slow. The people who talked about you behind your back were the same ones who'd bring you homemade chicken soup when you were sick. They didn't murder each other in cold blood.

"I could stand a cold iced tea right about now," she told Eden. "What about you?"

Eden looked at her solemnly. What words did she know? Was she potty-trained? Did she sleep through the night? The unknowns weighed on Skye's chest, giving her a glimpse of what Nash might be in store for. She didn't welcome the sympathetic pang she felt on his behalf.

Grabbing the diaper bag and pocketing her keys, Skye

went inside. She turned on the foyer light and stopped, feeling like an intruder.

The Wilder family had clout. Their name was on the elementary school building and a street downtown. Growing up, she'd been jealous of Nash and his younger sister, Remi. They'd had everything she'd craved—stability, security and solid standing in the community. If her mother was to be believed, her family had enjoyed that, too, when her physician father was alive.

Your father's death ruined everything.

Shaking off the memory of her mother's slurred words, she passed the formal dining room and entered a living room that shared space with the kitchen and breakfast nook.

French doors led to a patio that overlooked the pastures and trees beyond the fence line.

The house had old bones. While there had been updates— the hardwood floors and farmhouse kitchen reflecting the current era—the personal items told the story of the Wilder clan. The wall beside the fireplace was a historical exhibit of their four generations on this land. There were framed magazine articles on the mantel featuring Nash's father and his various contributions to the community. She noticed the ranch's legacy was the focus, not the family members. In fact, there wasn't a single photo of Nash or Remi. No smiling family photos of Wes, Glory and the kids. She would've expected to see something about Nash's military achievements, at least.

"All right, sweet girl, let's check out this diaper bag."

She lowered Eden to the leather couch, sank onto the smooth cushion beside her and pulled out a sippy cup.

"Juice." Eden snagged it and tried to pry the cap off.

Startled, Skye watched her in silence for a few moments. "Let me get that for you."

Impatient, Eden took hold of it with both hands and started guzzling. The poor child was parched.

A door opened and closed. She heard what sounded like boots thudding on the floor and a faucet being turned on. Moments later, Nash emerged from the hallway beside the kitchen, strode into the living room and came to a stop by the bookshelf in the corner. His honey-blond hair had the telltale hat ring, the longer strands on top sliding limply onto his forehead.

Nash studied Eden, his hands fisting. "Did she witness the murder? Was she in danger?"

Her palms got clammy. She wouldn't soon forget Lucy's final moments or her run-in with the murderer. "Eden was asleep in the car. The EMTs checked her out and didn't find any cause for alarm."

"What happened to your head?"

Grimacing, she traced the crisp bandage. "The killer was inside the abandoned house when I got there. I discovered his hiding place, and we had a scuffle. Unfortunately, he got away."

His eyes narrowed. "What's being done to capture him?"

"In order to come up with suspects, we have to learn more about Lucy's current life. The Mayfield Crime Scene Unit is on its way to the house to collect evidence. We'll canvass the town, check security cameras and talk to people. Someone had to have seen something."

"What was she doing in Tulip? Why was she at that house?"

"Good questions. Another one you should be asking is why Lucy didn't see fit to include you in the birth and raising of your daughter."

Nash paled. His vivid blue eyes seemed to crackle with electricity. "We can't ask her now, can we?"

The hint of pain underscoring his deep voice was like a bucket of water tossed on her indignation. Beneath his military-honed austerity beat a heart that could experience human emotion. He wasn't a robot, she reminded herself.

"You should talk to Lucy's mom," he said. "The last time we were together, Lucy said she and Maeve hadn't patched up their relationship, but things might've changed since then."

"Hank is on his way there now."

Skye was grateful she didn't have to do the death notification or spring the news of a surprise granddaughter on Maeve...assuming Lucy had kept her in the dark, like Nash.

"How quickly can we arrange for a paternity test? And what happens to Eden while we wait for the results?"

"I'll call my contact at CPS and ask her to make a trip out tomorrow. She can administer the test. We should get the results in a day or two. Sheriff Hines requires his deputies to be certified for kinship and respite care. Chen wants her to stay with me in the meantime." Of course, the fact she would soon be homeless would change things. She had three days to pay her rent before the official court proceedings, and she had no way of doing that. "I'll go outside and make the call. Mind sitting with her?"

Looking grim, he slowly assumed her spot.

Her contact, Kathy, agreed to come midmorning tomorrow. Thanking her, Skye ended the connection and sent a text to Hank to update him. He immediately replied that he wished to speak with her and Nash. She returned to the living room.

Nash had unearthed a container of cereal puffs and had scooped some into his hand. He was holding them out to Eden, patiently watching as she picked one, popped it in her mouth and then repeated the process. She was struck by their resemblance.

Lucy had obviously loved Eden and taken good care of her. She was clean, well-fed and had the appearance of good health. Skye didn't know why Lucy hadn't included Nash in their lives, but Lucy had been clear about her final wishes.

Why had God ripped this young mother from her little girl?

Why had He taken Skye's mother and left her younger sister alive but not truly living in a facility up the road?

Why did He allow so much suffering and pain?

I simply don't understand You, God.

As usual, she didn't receive a reply.

Nash couldn't help but be relieved when the deputy returned.

"The appointment with CPS is set for tomorrow morning," Skye announced as she came back into the room. "I heard from Hank. He asked that I wait here until he's finished at Maeve's and can come and speak to us both." Smoothing her hand over her upswept hair, she consulted her watch. "I'm going to make a quick run to the Dollar General."

She was leaving him alone? "You do realize I have zero experience with toddlers. Human toddlers, I mean." On the ranch, he dealt with mischievous and unpredictable calves day in and day out, and he'd spent his days in the corps perfecting his shooting skills and plotting tactical maneuvers.

"There are only three diapers in her bag."

"She wears diapers?"

Skye sighed. "She's not in pull-ups, so I'm assuming Lucy hadn't started the potty-training process."

He stared at Eden, who continued to take puffs from his hand and stuff them into her mouth. That panicky feeling sneaked in again. What did he know about diapers? Or what to feed her, when to put her to bed, how often to bathe her…

Lord, I don't understand why Lucy kept our daughter's existence a secret. I'm not equipped for this mission.

He had nothing to offer anyone. Hadn't his father pounded that truth into his head often enough growing up?

You're not getting it, son. Why can't you do anything right? You're useless.

His time in the military had proved his father wrong. Nash had flourished during his service, thanks to the clear expectations and goals. Because of a friend's testimony, he'd also learned that God loved him and thought he had value. But he'd never managed to entirely silence the lessons Wes Wilder had instilled in him.

As soon as Skye left, Eden started bawling.

He offered her the stuffed bear, and she batted it away. More tears flowed. He bounced the toy in the air and made silly animal sounds. When that didn't appease her, he dug through the diaper bag and found a pacifier. She wrinkled her nose in a way that reminded him of Lucy.

Lucy, who'd been brutally attacked and left for dead, who'd clung to life long enough to tell someone about him.

Nash tucked his hands beneath the toddler's arms. "I'm going to pick you up now," he warned.

When she didn't react, he boosted her up. She was lighter than a tin bucket. Tucking her against his chest, he began to walk around the house, talking to her as if she understood every word. At first, she was stiff and miserable. Her tears gradually abated, and she relaxed in his arms.

He continued to carry her around for the next hour, afraid to stop lest she dissolve into tears again. His most trusted ranch hand, Hardy, who'd been in his family's employ since Nash was a teenager, walked in unannounced and stopped dead in his tracks.

"Have I walked into the wrong house?" He rubbed his grizzled jaw in confusion, his smoky eyes popping wide. "Did I succumb to heatstroke?"

"This isn't really the time, Hardy."

"The boys won't believe this tale. I need a photograph for proof." He started to take out his old-model flip phone.

"Don't you dare."

Hardy sauntered over in his socks and peered at Eden. "Little filly looks an awful lot like your sister when she was runnin' around here in pigtails."

"There's a strong possibility she's mine."

"Hmm. And the mother?"

"Lucy Ackerman," he admitted, hardly able to wrap his head around the loss. "She's dead."

Hardy's humor vanished. "I'm right sorry to hear it." He cleared his throat. "Thought you should know the cows are where they're supposed to be. Santi and Dax punched out for the day."

"Thanks."

"You, uh, need me to stick around?"

Hardy was practically family. That was the only reason he'd offered, and he clearly hoped Nash would say no.

"Deputy Saddler is coming back."

"Hmm."

Hardy didn't offer his opinion on many things, and this time wasn't any different.

After Hardy left, Eden wiggled out of his arms and

began an inspection of the house. His relief was immense when Skye returned.

Nash hurried to greet her. She came through the living room and into the kitchen area to place the bags on the counter. "How did she do?"

"We managed."

Skye withdrew a pack of diapers, wet wipes and banana-flavored snacks from the bag. Her hair was damp around the temples, and the knot was barely containing the weight of her curls.

Eden entered the kitchen, held up her arms to Skye and grunted.

Skye's green eyes widened. After a quick glance at Nash, she lifted the toddler into her arms and smiled.

Nash had trouble breathing. The curve of Skye's lips, punctuated by her pearl-white teeth, brightened her entire face.

"I've got steaks ready to grill for supper." He opened the fridge door to distract himself. "There are assorted vegetables and yeast rolls in the freezer. Will any of that work for her?"

"We can try. I picked up some jars of baby food, just in case."

She lowered Eden and washed her hands. "I'll get started on the sides."

He paused at the laundry room door and turned back. She caught him watching her.

"If that's okay with you, of course."

"Of course it is. I just, uh, wanted to thank you."

"For what?"

"Being here."

Her look skewered him. "I'm not here for your sake."

The reminder reinstated the wall of tension between them. She wouldn't be there if she'd had a choice.

He retreated to the rear patio and prayed while the steaks were cooking. By the time he'd finished, the sun had sunk below the horizon, and the lights from the house spilled invitingly into the night. He carried the platter inside and was greeted with the cheerful sounds of a kids' show and the scent of fresh-baked rolls.

The table was set for three. Skye had discovered serving bowls in the recesses of his cabinets and placed the side dishes into them. Eden was already seated, her attention on the large television.

The scene had a surreal quality. Instead of eating alone in his silent house, he was about to have dinner with someone who wasn't a fan and a toddler who might be his daughter.

His desire to pray before the meal seemed to startle Skye, but she closed her eyes and bowed her head. He kept it brief, asking for God's protection and the quick resolution of Lucy's case. Afterward, Skye focused on assisting Eden.

His appetite dulled, Nash watched the process and wondered if he'd soon be on his own with Eden. He was grateful for the television program running in the background. It made the silence slightly less awkward. The first time he'd had dinner with a woman in years, and he couldn't think of a single thing to say.

After they'd eaten and cleaned up, Nash told her he was going to get something from his truck. He prayed Hank would get here soon so that Skye could take Eden home with her. He needed time and space to think.

After turning on the porch light, he walked to the rear of the truck and lifted the trifold cover. A crack split the air, and a bullet embedded itself in his bumper. He dived for cover, even as his mind rejected the implications. There had to be a logical explanation. Why would anyone shoot at him? On his own property, no less? But a second gun report blasted through the air, scattering gravel near his boots.

Someone was playing a deadly game—and he was the target.

THREE

Nash was pinned down, and he didn't have a gun on him. Skye cracked open the door.

"Come inside! I'll cover you."

"Where's Eden?"

She checked over her shoulder. Eden had stayed on the couch, just as she'd instructed. "Safe."

He squinted into the distant pastures, calm and steady. His military experience was showing. Staying low to the ground, he crawled toward the porch.

Skye turned off the light, eased through the opening and, Glock held high, darted behind the nearest post. A shot rang out and splintered the corner. Nash dived next to her on the porch, panting and gripping his hat.

His shoulder nudged her. "You okay?"

"Fine and dandy. Get your behind inside, cowboy. I've already called this in."

He gave a clipped nod. As he made for safety, another shot rang out. Skye returned fire. Sweat dampened her collar and the wood bit into her back as she waited for the next onslaught. When none came, she peered into the darkness, unable to see much of anything where the vegetable garden and greenhouse were located. The shots had likely come from the pine trees in the front pasture... a well-chosen spot. Good cover and close to the road.

The light behind the windows was acting like a spotlight for the shooter. She waited another five minutes before returning inside. "I can't see anything out there."

Nash approached, clutching Eden protectively in his arms. "Tulip hasn't seen trouble like this in years. First Lucy. Now this."

"Are you having a spat with any of your neighbors?"

"No. In fact, I'm about to purchase a parcel of Zane's land."

The Chesterfield ranch abutted Nash's and rivaled his in size. However, Zane didn't have the weight of history behind him. He'd left the corporate world while in his twenties and purchased the ranch.

"I've heard rumblings about financial problems in the wake of the fires." The Chesterfields had lost all of their chicken houses last year. "Is that why he's willing to part with some of it?"

"He needs an infusion of cash to keep the creditors off his back. I'm aiming to expand my operations. If I'm going to buy more cows, I'll need more land to support them. There's property for sale in the county, but it goes without saying Zane's is the best situated."

Skye didn't see a clear cause for hostility. Nash had a reputation for being fair in his business dealings.

"Have you angered anyone? Your animals become a problem?"

"Nothing beyond the usual." He paced the length of the couch, staying away from the windows. "Neighbors stick together for the good of the community. We help each other out. Barter chores and lend supplies. Hardy and I were at Zane's last week helping him move cows to another pasture. In return, he let me borrow a tractor."

"Well, someone has a burr under their saddle." She returned to the foyer as car lights cut through the shadows. "Hank is here."

Although Skye suspected the shooter was long gone, she ventured outside again to provide cover for Hank.

Wiping his bald head with a folded handkerchief, the deputy greeted Nash and Eden with a hearty hello. His forehead glistened and there were sweat patches on the uniform fabric stretching over his paunch. Bachelor Hank Flowers was old enough to be her dad. He was kind to everyone and had a fuse that was slow to ignite. He was beloved by Tulip's citizens.

"I didn't see anyone along the roadway," he said. "Of course, it'd be easy for someone to hide in the woods, out of sight."

"Nash can't name anyone who might have a grudge against him." After holstering her weapon, she led the group into the living room.

"We'll do a thorough search for casings at first light," he said.

"Agreed." She sank onto the couch, her headache starting up again with a vengeance. "Get us up to speed on Lucy's case?"

Nash sank onto the recliner. Eden seemed content to stay with him.

Hank tucked his handkerchief into his back pocket. His usually sparkly eyes were sad. "She was stabbed fourteen times. They didn't find the knife, her cell phone or any other personal items in the house."

Skye clenched her fists. "The violence suggests rage. This was probably someone who knew her."

"Were there any clues at all?" Nash asked.

"They've set up spotlights around the property in order to search the woods. Problem is, local teens use that house and the woods as their place to party unsupervised." When Nash pinched the bridge of his nose in obvious frustration, Hank held up his hand. "Don't get discouraged. We just have to have faith and patience."

Skye clung to hope. "Chen said reporters from several counties are already camped out around the house. The story will surely generate tips."

Although, she knew from experience that most didn't pan out, and sorting through them took time and manpower.

There was a knock on the door, and her fingers immediately went to her gun. While she was an officer of the law, she wasn't accustomed to this level of danger. One murder and an attempted murder so close together simply wasn't the norm in their neck of the woods. She didn't believe in coincidences, but she couldn't jump to conclusions, either.

Sergeant Chen stood on the other side of the door. He beckoned her and Hank outside with an impatient flick of his fingers. They moved to the side of the house, out of gunshot range.

"I came to discuss our plan of action. The townspeople are already on pins and needles with the news of Ackerman's death. We need to contain this latest wrinkle as best we can. With Sheriff Hines out of town, it falls to the three of us to keep everyone safe, and part of that is trying to avoid mass panic. Saddler, I want you to take point here with Nash and Eden."

"Protective custody?"

"Round the clock."

Her fingernails bit into her palms. "We do have a county to protect, in addition to identifying Lucy's killer and the person who has a grudge against Nash."

"This arrangement will work out for you," Chen sniped. "I heard about your eviction."

Already? Heat shot into her face. "I'm not irresponsible—" She stopped short of pouring out the reasons for her predicament.

Chen's upper lip curled. "This is going to reflect poorly on the department. Sheriff isn't going to be pleased. If I were you, I'd be ready to find another position."

Hank shifted his bulk toward her. "Sheriff Hines isn't going to sack anyone. He knows Skye is worth her weight in gold."

"You heard about it, too?"

He looked uncomfortable. "At the café."

Skye swallowed a groan. The news was circulating more quickly than she'd anticipated.

The deputy told Chen about their plans to search Nash's property in the morning. "We may find something useful."

Chen dismissed the suggestion. "We don't have time to deal with a disgruntled neighbor. Hank, you and I are going to canvass the eating establishments and gas stations in and around town. Someone must've seen Lucy yesterday."

Skye stepped forward. "The attack on Nash could be linked to Lucy's murder."

"Leave the sleuthing to a more experienced deputy." He waved her off like a pesky fly.

After he was back in his cruiser, she resisted the urge to stomp her foot.

Nash Wilder wasn't her favorite person, and now she was to stick to him like glue for the foreseeable future.

Nash looked as if he could chew barbed wire and spit it out. Skye could commiserate. They were both sleep-deprived. Eden had fussed throughout the night, obviously frightened and missing her mama. They'd taken turns walking her, holding her, even singing to her. At some point, Nash and Eden had fallen asleep in the recliner, and Skye had dozed on the couch.

The matter of paternity added a layer of tension. The test had been conducted at the sheriff's office. They'd had the place to themselves—Tulip's department consisted of Sheriff Hines, Sergeant Chen, Deputy Flowers and herself. There wasn't room in the budget for a receptionist. Her CPS contact, Kathy, had displayed her usual composure, but Nash had been as taut as a bowstring. Now they were about to face Lucy's mother, which wasn't going to be easy for a variety of reasons.

Hank had opted not to mention Eden to Maeve last night because she'd been so distraught. She hadn't asked about her granddaughter at all, which led Skye to believe Lucy hadn't told her, either.

"Wait here," she told Nash.

He shifted closer to a wicker chair on the deep veranda, out of sight of the door. He balanced Eden against his chest with one arm and held his Stetson in the other.

Skye walked to the entrance and pressed the doorbell. When Maeve opened the door, she had to work to keep her expression neutral.

One of Tulip's pillars, Maeve Ackerman usually presented a polished facade to the world, with styled, shoulder-length hair, flawless makeup—even in the height of summer—and boutique outfits with coordinated jewelry. The death of her only child had chiseled cracks in her Southern belle veneer. Maeve's round face was bare and splotchy, her eyes bloodshot, her nose red.

"Skye, honey, what are you doing here?" Her brow creased, and her blue eyes watered. "Did you find him? Did you find the man who took my daughter from me?"

"I'm afraid we don't have any suspects yet."

Her ringless fingers tightened around a wad of tissues. Her nail polish had been partially scraped off.

"I understand last night's news came as a shock, and I thought we could talk some more about Lucy. First, I want to reassure you that Eden is fine," she said, carefully observing her reaction.

Maeve's face reflected genuine confusion. "Who's Eden?"

"You weren't aware that Lucy had a daughter?"

She blinked. "Daughter? You must be mistaken. Lucy and I had our problems, but she wouldn't have kept a secret that huge from me."

Skye's tension ebbed. Maeve hadn't blocked Nash from being a father. That would make the situation slightly less complicated.

She glanced over her shoulder. "Nash?"

He stepped around the corner. After a beat, Maeve gasped. Her hands crept up to cover her mouth.

"Maeve, meet your granddaughter."

Nash stood statue-still under the other woman's inspection. Holding tightly to her stuffed bear, Eden sucked in her lower lip. They'd given her a bath that morning and dressed her in the only other clothes among her belongings, a pink shirt and jean shorts.

Maeve reverently touched Eden's cheek. "I—I don't understand. How can this be?" Her gaze punched Nash. "Did you know? Did you and Lucy conspire together to—"

"No and no," he gravely stated. "I found out yesterday."

"He's involved because Lucy named him as Eden's father," Skye explained. "You can see the resemblance?"

"She has Wilder eyes."

"We'll share the paternity results with you as soon as we receive them."

When a neighbor jogged by with her dog and did a double take, Skye motioned toward the door. "Maybe we should take this inside?"

"Yes, of course. Do come in." Maeve led them into the sprawling home that was located on a generous corner lot in the finest neighborhood in town. The sumptuous living room looked like a feature in *Southern Living* magazine.

"Can I get you some iced tea? Lemonade?"

Nash immediately declined. Skye asked for tea, recognizing the task would give Maeve a chance to gather her composure.

He set his Stetson atop a cushioned chair and circled around to the sofa table where several picture frames were placed between a lamp and assorted knickknacks.

"Mama!"

Eden pointed to the frame on the end and repeated the word. Nash's troubled gaze shot to Skye. She went to stand beside him and picked up the photo—an informal snapshot of Lucy, looking happy and carefree. When Lucy was in high spirits, she drew others to her like moths to a light bulb. She could make a dreary day festive, make a boring task exciting, make problems melt away…at least for a little while.

Skye, Lucy and their friend Jama had been as tight as sisters during high school. Skye had thought nothing could change that. She supposed every high school senior thought the same. Her vision blurred, and she set down the frame.

Maeve returned with slim, frosted glasses and handed one to Skye. She kept the other for herself, although she put hers on the end table without taking a drink. She sat in the floral-print chair kitty-corner to the sofa and beckoned them to take a seat. Nash and Skye settled on the cushions, leaving plenty of space between them. Eden was content to remain on his lap.

Skye took a long sip of the sweet tea. "Is Virgil on his way home?"

"He's flying in tonight."

Lucy's stepdad spent more time traveling for work than he did in Tulip.

"My sister's also coming in to help with funeral arrangements."

Skye took out her notebook and pen. "Maeve, when was the last time you spoke with Lucy?"

"I—I told Hank this already. About six months ago. She called me, and we had a nice conversation. She seemed settled. Happy." She couldn't stop staring at Eden. "Lucy didn't mention I had a granddaughter." She radiated grief and confusion. "I would've helped her."

"Did she happen to mention where she was living?"

Her gaze swerved to Skye. "As a matter of fact, I have her address. I offered to send her some money, and she accepted." She retrieved a paper from a mahogany hutch and gave it to Skye.

"Biloxi. That's not far."

"An hour and a half," Nash said, his jaw hard. "Two, tops."

Maeve leaned forward in her chair. "What went on between you and Lucy? Are you the reason she kept Eden a secret?"

Splotches of red crept up his neck. "I admit that I wasn't always a gentleman when it came to your daughter, but I didn't drive her away. I would've taken care of her and Eden if she'd given me the chance." He smoothed Eden's hair.

Maeve stewed on that. "I went to her apartment sev-

eral days after she called me. I just wanted to see her."
Her voice cracked, and she dabbed at her nose with the
tissues. "She wasn't home. Her roommate refused to let
me in or tell me where she was."

"What was the roommate's name?"

"Tara Lane."

"Did you go back and try again?"

"I was tempted to, of course, but I figured she wouldn't
appreciate me horning in on her new life. I decided to
wait for her to reach out again. Let it be her decision."

"Was Lucy seeing anyone?"

"If she was, she didn't mention it. She talked about her
job at a clothing shop. I'm sorry—I don't recall the name."

"Do you know if she was having trouble at work?"

"No, I don't." She reached up to worry her pearls, only
to realize she wasn't wearing any. "I'm sorry I can't be
more helpful."

Skye closed her notebook. "You've given me enough
to start. Thanks for speaking with us."

After downing the rest of the tea, she stood. Nash
did, too.

Maeve spread her hands. "I'd be happy to keep Eden
here with me until the results come in."

Nash threaded his fingers through his hair. Every time
he did, the longer strands slid right back onto his forehead. "I appreciate the offer, but she's comfortable at the
ranch. She's used to me and Deputy Saddler. I don't want
to upset her world again so soon."

When the older woman looked as if she might protest,
Skye intervened. "You've got a lot on your shoulders right
now, Maeve. We wouldn't want to add to your responsibilities. I'm sure you and Nash can work something out
once the dust settles."

Not wanting to worry the woman further, Skye didn't

add that she was under orders to stay with both Nash and Eden.

Maeve relented, although she didn't look happy about it. Skye couldn't blame her. It stood to reason she'd take comfort in her granddaughter's company.

Once they were back out at Nash's heavy-duty truck, which probably cost more than Skye's yearly salary, he buckled Eden in and climbed behind the wheel.

"You're good at managing conversations, Deputy. Do you maneuver people, too?"

"Like cattle?" A bubble of laughter emerged.

"You know what I mean."

"Part of my job is knowing how to avoid confrontations. Keep the peace, and all that."

"And running down a killer? Do you have what it takes?"

"Trust me," she told him firmly, "Lucy's murderer won't go unpunished."

FOUR

Nash was acutely aware they were causing a stir in the grocery aisles. A man and woman who didn't typically share more than a civil nod were sharing a buggy and were in the company of a small child no one had set eyes on before. He gritted his teeth, then worked to relax his jaw. He was going to put himself in the dentist's chair, if he wasn't careful.

He watched as Skye studied the price labels of the different cereal puff brands. She was prolonging this excursion because she insisted on searching for the least expensive choice of every item on their list. Except for diapers. She insisted those weren't something to be skimped on. He'd reassured her that he could and would foot the bill.

She wasn't terrible company, he had to admit. He'd learned more about her in the past twenty-four hours than he had in a lifetime of living in the same zip code. She had a decent singing voice and a hearty appetite. After leaving Maeve's, they'd had lunch at the Pit Stop. The downtown fixture had the best coconut cream pie in the state, and he ate there at least once a week. Skye's initial reluctance had melted when he'd offered to pay, and she'd ordered a triple-stack burger topped with their famous onion rings and a strawberry milkshake.

Adding a container of apple-flavored puffs to the growing collection of supplies, she tapped her chin. "They don't have clothes here, and she has two outfits to her name. Mayfield has an organization that caters to the foster care community. We could go there for free clothes. Or there's the thrift store on Carter Street."

Nash thought about the pregnant cows that needed to be checked, the upcoming bull-riding event he was in charge of organizing and the host of other chores waiting on him. Hardy and the others were dependable, but he didn't like to heap everything onto them. "Let's go to the nearest store that sells kids' clothes and get enough to tide her over."

Skye agreed. "If for some reason the test returns negative, I'll see if a CPS-affiliated organization will reimburse you."

He looked down at Eden, who sat quietly in the buggy's top seat, her feet swinging. He wasn't sure what he hoped the test would reveal. If it was negative, Eden would likely go to Maeve while CPS searched for her biological father. He already felt protective of her, but he wasn't the best person to raise her. He could provide for her material needs. Food, clothing, shelter. Everything else? The messy stuff that really mattered? He wasn't so sure.

Skye's shoulders bunched and dread slid into her eyes. He turned toward the other end of the aisle to see what had caused the reaction. Matilda Carlson, a Tulip native of seventy-plus years, bustled toward them, her bowling-ball-sized purse swinging from her arm.

"Skye, you poor dear. I spoke with your neighbor, Beverly, this morning. She's distraught over your situation. She—"

"Afternoon, Matilda," Skye interrupted. "How's Ace?"

Matilda blinked at Nash and Eden. Ace was her beloved miniature schnauzer, and she took him everywhere, usually in his very own stroller.

"He's at the groomer getting handsome. Listen, I want you to know, you're welcome to stay with me for as long as you want. Beverly talked to Lewis on your behalf, but he wouldn't budge. Shameful, a landlord kicking a deputy out of her home."

Kicked out of her home?

Skye refused to look at him. Her gaze was pinned to the shiny tiles beneath their feet like she was wishing she could sink through them.

"Skye?" His prompt was ignored.

"Thank you for your concern, Matilda." Lifting Eden from the buggy, she mumbled, "We'll be out in the truck."

Nash handed Skye the diaper bag and his truck keys, and she hurried out of the store.

"Poor dear," Matilda said, shaking her head. "Beverly agreed to store her most prized belongings for the time being, but Lewis will donate her furniture if she doesn't remove it."

Nash extricated himself from the conversation. His mind was spinning as he paid the cashier and unloaded the bags into the truck bed and refastened the cover. Behind the wheel once more, he turned the radio off and angled toward her.

"What's going on?"

Staring out the passenger window, she gave a half shrug. "I couldn't keep up with my rent."

He waited for further explanation, but it didn't come.

How could this have happened? The cruiser was her only vehicle, and it was paid for by the county. She lived in a modest apartment complex without expensive amenities. Maybe she had credit card debt? She seemed careful about money, but maybe that was a result of her current state of affairs.

He admitted he knew very little about Skye's personal life. Back in school, it was common knowledge that she hadn't had an easy home life. Anita Saddler had become a slave to the bottle after her husband's death, leaving Skye to care for herself and her younger sister, Dove. Nash had been in boot camp when news about the Saddler tragedy reached him. Anita had driven drunk one night with the girls in the car. She'd wrapped her car around a telephone pole and died upon impact. Dove, tossed from the wreckage, remained in a vegetative state to this day. Skye had walked away with only a broken arm.

On the way home, he pulled into the Dollar General. Skye agreed to take some cash from him and purchase a few outfits for Eden. She emerged a short time later with a single bag.

"Matilda seems to think your landlord will do whatever he pleases with your belongings if they aren't removed. I have a truck and a strong back, not to mention several employees who'd be willing to lend a hand. We can do it this evening."

Her lips parted. "You'd do that for me?"

"Moving furniture is nothing compared to what you're doing for me and Eden."

"I don't have anywhere to store it."

"I do. You can keep it on the ranch."

Skye assessed him, which gave him ample opportunity to appreciate her unique beauty without excuse. Her clear green eyes, framed by sleek brows, contrasted with her rich dark skin. They were the prettiest, most captivating eyes he'd ever seen.

"I'll take you up on that offer," she said at last, her thick lashes sweeping down and shutting him out.

He shook his head to clear it. He couldn't let himself forget why they were suddenly in each other's back pockets—there was a murderer loose in their town and they just might be next on his list.

Seated in the backhoe the following morning, Nash dug a grave for the newborn calf they'd discovered in the pasture earlier. While they tried to keep track of the pregnant cows, sometimes one wandered off and encountered trouble in the birthing process. The gentle sunshine and birdsong did little to lift his mood.

He couldn't shake his sadness over Lucy's death. He was sad for Lucy and everything she would miss in her daughter's life. Sad for Maeve, who'd tried hard to help Lucy. He was sad for Eden, of course, and maybe a little for himself.

Eden was a reminder of the good times he'd shared with Lucy. The toddler's presence had unearthed memories of the past, and he was remembering things he'd buried or believed discarded.

He'd known Lucy Ackerman his whole life. Born a month apart, they'd entered kindergarten together, and because Tulip had one elementary, middle and high school, they'd sat in the same classes year after year.

There had been no reason for them to interact outside of class. She'd been a popular cheerleader, and he a cowboy more interested in ranching, hunting and fishing than sports. He'd occasionally attended the games and bonfires with his best friends William and Hugo. Not because they had been inspired by school spirit, but because there'd been little for teenagers to do in Tulip.

During their sophomore year, Lucy had approached

him after the homecoming game. He'd been surprised and flattered by her attention, and they'd soon become an item. She was his first girlfriend, and he'd quickly learned how inept he was at being a boyfriend. Lucy's friend Skye had noticed right away. Fast-forward a decade or so, and Skye now had a front-row seat to his poor fathering skills.

The results of that paternity test couldn't come fast enough.

Out of the corner of his eye, he registered a rider approaching. Hardy and Santi, who'd been observing Nash's progress from their saddles, swiveled to watch the latecomer.

Nash turned off the backhoe and climbed down. Nudging his hat up, he frowned at Dax.

"Nice of you to join us," he drawled.

Dax pulled up on the reins and walked his palomino closer. "Sorry, boss. Ma's arthritis has been acting up again."

Nash knew Dax's mama. She'd suffered from poor health for years. He also knew Dax had a string of young ladies drooling over him. In his midtwenties, Dax was enjoying the single life to the fullest.

"Were you really at your mama's bedside?" Santi smirked. "Or with your latest girlfriend?"

Dax's eyes flashed, but he didn't respond. Santi was older and more experienced, and Dax was intimidated by him.

"Listen up, boys. It's time to leave the fun and games behind, because we have a real problem on our hands. You've all heard about the shooter on the ranch. Deputy Saddler is going to stick around until we get answers. I want you to stay vigilant. Anything seems off, call me immediately. If you see someone who doesn't belong on the ranch, don't engage them. Get to a safe spot."

The hands nodded in agreement. After they buried the calf, he left them to their respective tasks and returned to the house.

Entering through the utility room, he was greeted with delightful scents that reminded him of his childhood and laid-back weekend mornings. His mom, Glory, had done a week's worth of baking every Saturday, and she'd generously doled out samples to him and Remi.

Skye's singsong voice, followed by Eden's giggles, dissolved those thoughts.

Nash quickly washed his hands and entered the kitchen. Skye was stationed beside the stove. Eden was perched on the counter, nibbling on a waffle and bouncing up and down.

With one hand steadying Eden, Skye dragged her own waffle through a rivulet of maple syrup on a plate, took an exaggerated bite and hummed in her throat. Eden giggled and scrunched her nose.

Nash's breath caught in his chest. His house hadn't seen this sort of domestic scene for years, certainly not since his mom's death.

Skye noticed him, and a startled expression stole over her face, as if she'd been caught with her hand in the cookie jar. The official uniform, badge and weapon had been exchanged for a soft white cotton shirt, khaki shorts and slide-on tennis shoes. Her ebony curls had been released from their usual restrictive style to fall to her shoulders. She was a strikingly beautiful woman, and she looked like any other mom feeding her daughter breakfast.

He hadn't thought of Skye like this before, and it did strange things to his equilibrium.

"Um, are you hungry?" she asked.

His gaze locked on the ancient waffle maker plugged into the wall. "I didn't know I owned one of those."

"Oh, this is mine."

He stepped closer, and Eden smiled at him, revealing tiny baby teeth. She held out her piece of waffle, and his heart melted.

Lord, I think I'm in trouble. What if the test proves I'm not her father?

Wouldn't that be for the best?

He was shocked to discover his mind and heart weren't exactly in agreement.

As Skye poured more batter on the waffle maker, he surveyed the counter. "Did you put blueberries in there?"

"I found some in the freezer. Hope you don't mind."

"I meant it when I said make yourself at home."

Last night, as he and the guys had emptied her apartment, she'd been openly embarrassed. There'd also been a streak of defensiveness evident in her demeanor, as if she'd dared them to judge her. He'd hurried the process along, not making any personal remarks or asking any questions. He'd wanted to spare her humiliation, which was progress, considering he might've rubbed it in when they were younger.

"Can you watch her? I'll get you a plate." She padded over to the fridge, and he tried not to stare at her long, shapely legs.

"Milk or juice?"

"Milk, please." He stood directly in front of Eden. "I guess she needs a high chair."

"She'll need a lot of things. Crib, mattress, dresser, training potty."

He tried not to panic. The ranch was doing well financially, and he could afford to buy her furniture. It was the rearranging of his life that overwhelmed him. Who would watch her while he worked the ranch?

"Have you spoken to Remi?" Skye poured milk into a beveled glass.

"I'm waiting until I have something concrete to share."

She removed the waffle, which had turned a lovely golden hue, and placed it on a plate. "Here you go."

"Why don't we take this to the table?"

"Sure. Eden can sit in my lap."

When they were settled, he said grace and dug in. He couldn't suppress a groan.

Skye smiled. "Good, aren't they?"

"Light as air. Perfect sweetness."

"I'm glad you approve, because I eat them a lot. You'd be surprised how versatile they are."

"I won't complain."

"They're my grandma's recipe. Dove loved them. Begged me to make them every day before school." Her smile faded. Blinking fast, she covered the awkward moment with a long sip of her coffee.

He remembered the youngest Saddler sister, of course, but she'd been four years younger. Far enough behind them in school that he hadn't seen her often. She'd been the quieter of the two, if he recalled correctly.

Nash set down his fork. "How is she?"

Cutting another portion for Eden, she shrugged one shoulder. "There's not much change from day to day."

He hadn't stopped to consider Skye's struggles—past or present. She presented a commanding, capable air to the world. He realized it was a mask to cover the pain.

"Do you see her often?"

"Once a week. Usually Sunday afternoons." She cleared her throat. "Is your sister still working in Atlanta?"

"Yes. I miss having her around, but she's happy where she is."

"I always liked her."

Three years his junior, Remi had been close enough in age to share some of the same friends. After their mother's death, Remi had leaned on him. Their father certainly hadn't been capable of comforting his children.

With a start, he realized he and Skye had some major life events in common. They'd both lost one parent when they were young and were raised by the one left behind—both had been ill-equipped for the job.

"A shame you can't say the same about me," he murmured.

Her green eyes shot to his as she opened her mouth to respond. A message notification distracted her.

"The toxicology report is in." She set the phone down. "Lucy was clean."

He blew out a breath, his gaze going to Eden. How had Lucy conquered her addictions and when? How had she supported herself through the pregnancy and after the birth? There were so many unanswered questions.

"What are you doing today?"

"I'm to stay with you and Eden, per Chen's orders."

"Did he say you couldn't leave town?"

"He didn't give specifics."

"What do you say we drive down to Biloxi?"

Her eyes gleamed. "Chen said he'd ask Biloxi PD to check Lucy's current address, but I'd rather do it myself. It's not that far. Can you get away from the ranch?"

There was always something to do at the ranch, but this was important. "I'll leave Hardy in charge."

She smoothed Eden's hair. "I'm not sure taking her

with us is the best idea. You never know what we might find. Maybe Maeve will agree to watch her."

Nash prayed Biloxi held answers instead of more questions.

FIVE

Skye's impatience to get on the road was thwarted, and she was reminded that toddlers and cattle couldn't be rushed. While she bathed and dressed Eden—a task that took longer than expected—Nash had to help Hardy wrangle a stubborn cow out of a pond. Nash had wound up in said pond, and he'd had to shower for the second time that day. Then Eden had announced she was ready for lunch by tugging on the fridge door and grunting. By the time they'd dropped her off at Maeve's and arrived in Biloxi's outskirts, it was almost suppertime.

Nash parked his truck against the curb opposite a non-descript duplex with white shutters and trim. After killing the engine, he rested his hands on his thighs. There was a fresh scrape across his knuckles, and his watch face was cracked. He'd changed into another Western-style shirt, this one aqua and white. A pristine white Stetson sat on the seat between them.

She was beginning to notice little things about him, which felt strange.

"This is it, right?"

Skye double-checked the map directions on her phone. "Yep. According to the house numbers, it's the one on the left."

The duplex units shared one driveway, and a single vehicle was parked there. The sun had dipped behind the building, casting shadows on the front lawn.

"Decent neighborhood," Nash remarked.

She glanced through the windshield. This area wasn't new and shiny. However, the modest homes were mostly well maintained.

"Someone's coming out of her apartment." Sitting up taller, he grabbed the handle. "A woman. Let's go talk to her."

She grasped his forearm, and her words fizzled on her tongue. His skin was sprinkled with fine blond hair and hot to the touch. He turned his head, and she found his blue eyes almost blinding.

Jerking her fingers away, she ducked her head, letting her hair become a shielding curtain. She caught a glimpse of herself in the side mirror and grimaced. She'd forgone the bandage, and the scabbed-over cuts near her hairline were not attractive.

Since when do you care about others' opinions of your appearance?

"Let me go first."

"Worried she's going to wallop me with the garbage bag?"

Mumbling under her breath, Skye exited the truck, tucked her phone in her jeans' pocket and tugged her shirt over her holster. He got out, plopped his Stetson on his head and waited for her to round the hood. Together, they crossed the street. A lawn mower buzzed in the distance, and a jogger huffed by with his dog.

The young woman hefted the bag into the garbage can and let the lid slam shut. She started to retrace her steps and then seemed to notice their approach. Of medium height and build, she had short, straight brown hair and was dressed in exercise gear and sneakers.

"Good morning," Skye called out, flashing her badge. "Do you have a minute?"

A wary expression took hold, and she glanced around as if she expected to see a police cruiser. As they got nearer, Skye introduced herself.

"I'm Deputy Skye Saddler, and this is Nash Wilder. Is this Lucy Ackerman's residence?"

"Lucy's my roommate," she said, looking them up and down. "She's not here."

Skye and Nash exchanged a look. "What's your name?"

"Tara Lane."

"Do you mind if we talk inside, Tara?"

"I guess."

They entered a combined living and dining area. The walls were soft white, punctuated with floral prints and an amateur painting of the sea. Jade green pillows were propped around the sectional couch, and a plush blanket was folded in the corner. Nash homed in on the bright pink baby bouncer in the corner, and she felt the odd urge to rub his back in consolation.

Tara turned one of the chairs at the table around and sat, gesturing for them to take the couch. Skye perched on a cushion, but Nash didn't move.

"When was the last time you spoke to Lucy?"

"Tuesday morning. Why? Is something wrong?"

"I'm sorry to say she was murdered."

Tara clapped her hand over her mouth, her gray eyes popping wide.

A muscle in Nash's jaw twitched. "We're trying to find her killer. To do that, we need information. Will you help us?"

She lowered her hand. "Where's Eden? Is she okay?"

"She's safe."

Tara went limp. "I'll help you. I—I just can't believe this. Lucy…gone. How? Why?"

"We can't discuss the details of the case," Skye replied.

Tara's reaction seemed genuine. Unlike Chen, who'd worked with the Jackson PD, Skye didn't have experience with hard-core criminals. She was pretty good at detecting when someone was lying, though.

Nash finally took a seat beside Skye, rubbing his palms slowly over his jeans. His strong body radiated coiled tension.

"She was in a good mood that morning," Tara offered without prompting. "She said she was going home. I knew that meant Tulip."

Skye had failed to bring her notebook, so she opened the notes app on her phone. "Did she say why? Or who she was meeting?"

"I only know she had a friend there. A man. She didn't share his name."

"A boyfriend?"

"No, not him. She hinted there was someone special in her life. Someone else."

Nash shifted impatiently. "Why didn't she share details? You weren't close?"

She shrugged. "I moved in five months ago. We have a mutual friend, and I needed somewhere quick to land. Lucy and I worked opposite shifts and didn't have a lot of time to hang out."

Skye decided to switch topics. "How was Lucy with Eden?"

"Eden is Lucy's whole world. They're rarely apart. She even left the Crab Pot for a job with less pay so she could be with her."

Skye's fingers tapped out the details. Without looking up, she asked, "Current place of employment?"

"A New You Boutique. The owner is nice. She let Lucy set up a play area for Eden."

"What about Eden's father?" Skye prompted, lifting her gaze.

Tara sighed. "He's not in the picture."

Nash grunted.

"Did Lucy say why?" Skye asked.

"No, and I didn't ask."

"Did Lucy talk about her mother? Maeve said she sent money to help out."

Tara frowned. "Like I said, we didn't have a whole lot of deep conversations." She threaded her fingers through her short, thick hair. "She did mention there was a problem with her stepdad."

"Virgil Ackerman?" She couldn't keep the surprise out of her voice. This was the first she'd heard of any issue with him.

"I guess."

Nash appeared as confused as Skye. They were both aware how difficult it was to keep secrets in Tulip. Plus, they had been in Lucy's inner circle.

"Did she say what the problem was?" he asked.

"No. I just got the impression she didn't like him."

Skye was eager to return to Tulip to dig into this news. "Tara, is there anyone you can think of who might've wanted to hurt Lucy? Someone she might've had an altercation with?" She gestured to the interior wall connecting the units. "Are you on friendly terms with the neighbors?"

"We say hello and occasionally gripe about the bad internet. That's it." She spread her hands wide. "I wish I had more information."

Skye pocketed her phone. "We appreciate your help. Do you mind if we take a look around?"

Tara pointed them in the direction of Lucy's room and went into her own, closing the door to give them privacy. Skye detoured into the kitchen, opening cabinets, drawers and, finally, the fridge.

"What are you hoping to find?" Nash said quietly, boots planted far apart on the worn linoleum.

She shrugged. "Anything that shouldn't be here. Or things that should be but aren't. As you can see, there are sippy cups, baby plates, applesauce pouches." She pointed to the fridge contents. "Juices for Eden. Sports drinks for Tara, and look at that." She tapped the pitcher of sweet iced tea.

His Adam's apple bobbed. "Lucy couldn't live without her sweet tea."

A bittersweet feeling stole over her. "She used to say it ran through her veins."

"I remember."

Skye sighed. "I regret not making an effort to stay in touch."

Nash didn't comment. Instead, he continued down the hall, opened the door to Lucy's bedroom and paused on the threshold. Skye brushed past him, her gaze trying to soak in everything at once. Pink bedspread. Fuzzy gold decorative pillows. Framed children's art above the metal headboard.

The room was crammed with furniture for Lucy and her child. The lone dresser wasn't large enough to hold their combined clothes, so she'd put Eden's things in pink-and-gray cloth boxes tucked into an open-faced cabinet. Skye opened the closet and sucked in a breath.

"What is it?" Nash quickly joined her.

She opened the door wider. The inner panels were

completely covered with old photographs from their school days. Nash reached out and touched one of himself and Lucy. She was dressed in her cheerleading uniform, and he had on his standard cowboy gear.

"Was that after a game?" she whispered.

He peered closer, bringing his face near hers. She got momentarily sidetracked by a scar on his cheekbone, a recent one that was almost healed. Ranch work was tough on the body, it seemed. He smelled like Dial soap and musky aftershave.

"Must be." He pointed to another one. "There's the six of us."

Nash, William and Hugo had been a tight trio. When Nash and Lucy became an item, she'd brought Skye and Jama into the circle, willingly or not. "We were babies."

They went quiet, searching the smiling faces and reliving times gone by.

She missed those innocent days. Even though her life had never been easy, thanks to her mom's penchant for losing her mind to drink, she'd had no idea what nightmare awaited her.

"Skye." His voice dipped as he pointed to a photo. "Look at this."

She felt like she was being strangled. "Dove."

Skye skimmed trembling fingers over the image of her and Dove, arms wrapped around each other, laughing at who knew what. She made a point not to look at the old photos she kept locked away in dusty boxes. It was too excruciating to remember life before the crash and how her sister used to be.

Vision swimming, she presented him with her back. Nash's hand came down on her shoulder and squeezed. She didn't know what surprised her more—the simple gesture of comfort or how much she appreciated it. Skye was so very alone in her sorrow. Her best friend, Honoria, would gladly listen and offer condolences, but Skye rarely burdened her. Honoria would want to pray with her and point her to appropriate scriptures. Skye wasn't ready to accept God's help. Her anger and hurt were as fresh as the night the doctors had told her Dove would never be the same. Nash was here and convenient, but she wasn't about to open up to him.

"Why don't you search the closet for clues?" she managed to say. "Also, see if there's a duffel or suitcase we can pack Eden's belongings in."

"Yes, ma'am," he said softly.

Skye searched the dresser drawers, ignoring the feeling that she was intruding. This was necessary to find Lucy's killer. Next, she checked under the bed. There were several flat containers with extra sheets and blankets, as well as winter clothes and coats.

"Looks like official papers in here," Nash said, setting an accordion file on the bed.

He withdrew last year's tax documents, the duplex rental contract and a recent smartphone receipt. When he pulled out Eden's birth certificate, he sank to the edge of the bed. The place for father's name was blank.

Skye pulled out the other papers. "Says she was seven pounds at birth."

She studied his expression. The protective mask had slipped, revealing his inner conflict. He looked torn between wanting to be Eden's dad and being terrified of the responsibility.

"What are you thinking?" she asked, silently imploring him to open up to her.

His jaw worked. "I'd like to find the name of Eden's pediatrician and pay them a visit. Her medical history is a complete mystery. What if she has medical issues?"

That wasn't the revelation she'd been hoping for. "I'll ask Tara if she knows anything. We can also check the bathroom and kitchen cabinets for medications. The other option is to ask Kathy to call them, because they won't divulge that information to us."

"Right." Returning the birth certificate to its slot, he stood. "I'm going outside to call Maeve."

Before she could speak, he strode out of the room and down the hall. The front door opened and closed.

Skye returned to the pictures, touching the one of Lucy and Nash. "Don't worry, Luce. Nash and I will make sure your daughter is safe and well."

The evasive cowboy was committed to Eden's well-being. Skye had a feeling that the paternity results—positive or negative—weren't going to change that.

After speaking with Maeve, who reassured him that Eden was doing fine, Nash navigated Biloxi's streets with the help of Skye's directions. Rush-hour traffic had thinned. He was disappointed they hadn't found definitive clues pointing to Lucy's murderer. One thing they had accomplished, however, was gathering Eden's belongings.

He glanced over at Skye. Since taking this bodyguard assignment, she'd started wearing casual clothes. She wasn't a fussy dresser. Today, she'd chosen a heather-gray, V-necked shirt, jeans and sneakers. The gun tucked against her waist was barely noticeable. Give her a Stetson, and she just might pass for a rancher.

"Were you aware of friction between Lucy and Virgil?" she asked.

"It's news to me."

"Me, too." She rested her phone in her lap and studied the passing businesses. "He and Maeve got married while Lucy was in middle school. Although he didn't formally adopt her, Maeve insisted she be known as Lucy Ackerman. He was around a whole lot more then. If he were aggressive or abusive, surely Lucy would've confided in someone."

"Why don't you reach out to Jama?" The soft-spoken redhead had been the calm to Skye's storm and the reason to Lucy's whimsy. "She's a librarian, I heard. Married to a lawyer and living in Houston."

"I'll call her when we get back. I'm also going to have a heart-to-heart with Virgil, but I prefer to do that in person."

Nash couldn't imagine the burly, introverted businessman murdering anyone, let alone his stepdaughter. But his military stint had taught him the line between self-control and unleashed rage was a thin one. Only Virgil, Maeve and Lucy knew what had really gone on in their home.

The boutique where Lucy worked was located in a stand-alone building and sandwiched between a nail salon and a cell phone store. The windows gleamed yellow in the gathering dusk.

He parked between the other two vehicles in the lot. Heat clung to the blacktop. Inside, a customer ducked into the fitting room, and an elegant, silver-haired lady greeted them.

Nash's attention zeroed in on the playpen behind the register. A forgotten stuffed animal was in it, and he could picture Lucy bending down and kissing Eden's head.

His gut churned, and his determination to find the person responsible for her death solidified. Whether or not they shared a child, he would seek justice for Lucy.

Skye touched his sleeve and he turned to her and the woman.

"This is Mrs. Calderwood, the owner. She said Lucy asked for a few days off."

The lady rested her clasped hands on the counter. "I didn't ask her reasons, of course." Her expression was pleasant and curious. "If you leave your number, I'll be sure to give it to her when she comes in."

He turned and caught Skye staring intently at the playpen, a dip in her forehead. Her job was not an easy one.

"I'm afraid I have some bad news," she said heavily.

Mrs. Calderwood listened with growing horror as Skye relayed the information. Dashing away tears, Lucy's boss insisted she had no useful information to impart. Lucy had mentioned having a love interest, but she hadn't shared anything beyond that.

Back in the heat of the truck cab, he started the engine and let the cool air flow over him.

Skye buckled in. "What do we know so far? Lucy regularly visited a male friend in Tulip, who she may or may not have been dating. Lastly, she and Virgil might've been at odds."

He sighed. "Nothing concrete, but at least it's something."

Beside him, Skye dug in a printed bag she'd brought along. "Hungry?"

She held out a plastic-wrapped waffle.

"Waffles for supper?"

"Waffle sandwiches," she corrected. "I found slices of ham, turkey and cheese in your fridge and made us these for the road." Her curls danced along her shoulder, and a necklace winked around her neck. "I also have carrot sticks."

His stomach rumbled as he accepted the sandwich. "You weren't kidding about the waffles, were you?"

"They're extremely versatile." She bit into hers and grinned. "These were left over from this morning. Can't let them go to waste."

Were her economical ways a product of her current circumstances? Or had she learned them as a young teen, thanks to her mom's drinking habit?

He bit into it, surprised he liked it. "This is good."

She smirked in triumph.

He'd finished his off and was reaching for his water bottle when his phone rang. His pleasure over the satisfying meal vanished.

"It's Kathy from CPS."

Skye lowered her sandwich to her lap, her gaze glued to him.

"Mr. Wilder?" Kathy's voice filtered through the phone's speaker. "We've got the results."

His heart was surely about to burst out of his chest. "Yes?"

"It's a positive match. You are Eden's biological father."

SIX

Nash hadn't uttered a single word since they'd left the boutique parking lot half an hour ago. The positive paternity results hadn't come as a surprise to Skye. Lucy had named him as her child's father. Sure, she could've lied out of desperation to secure Eden's future with the owner of a well-established ranch and cattle company. Skye might've considered that as a possibility if not for the toddler's obvious Wilder traits. Nash himself agreed her age fit the timeline of his and Lucy's brief reunion.

He must be in shock. After sharing the results with her, he'd retreated into himself, his attention 100 percent on the road. Lights from streetlamps and passing businesses flickered over his rigid features.

"Feel like stopping for coffee somewhere?" Maybe fresh air and a break from driving would revive him.

"Coffee isn't going to fix this."

"What's there to fix? I happen to think you've got what it takes to do right by Eden."

He dragged his gaze from the road to shoot her a look of disbelief. "Never figured on your vote of confidence. Thought I wasn't good enough for Lucy, so how can I be good enough for Eden?"

She inhaled, recalling the scathing letter she'd mailed

to Parris Island, where he'd been in boot camp for three months. He'd never mentioned receiving it, and now she hoped he hadn't.

"It wasn't that you weren't good enough. You're a Wilder, after all. That means something in our neck of the woods." He grunted in response. "I got the impression you didn't care about Lucy."

"You couldn't have been more wrong."

"How so?"

He gripped the steering wheel with both hands. His Stetson lay on the seat between them, and his hair had slid onto his forehead.

"Talk to me, Nash. We're adults. Those years are long gone."

"She was a lot to handle, okay?"

Skye nodded. "Lucy was unique."

"She was needy."

She curled her fingers. Released them. "Yes."

"I didn't know how to be what she needed." He ground out the admission.

Skye acknowledged she didn't have it all together in high school, either. Still didn't. "Did you talk to each other? Lucy used my shoulder for more than her fair share of crying jags during those days. She was head over heels for you, even though half the football players would've given up their spot on the team for one date with her. You kept her guessing. Was that deliberate?"

He unexpectedly made a turn off the state road onto a side street, and she braced her hand on the dash.

"Coffee is a good idea after all," he said.

There were several fast-food restaurants along this stretch of road, including a nationwide coffee chain. The buildings faced the busy route between Tulip and Biloxi.

Nash's eyes were wells of regret. Grief, too. Maybe it

was easy to believe he didn't have feelings because he was so skilled at burying them.

"I'm sorry. This isn't the time to grill you."

"You were a good friend to Lucy." He pushed his fingers through his honey-hued hair. "I'm glad she had you in her corner. I didn't mean to hurt her. Bottom line is I had no business dating anyone. I was a pro at messing up my own life. I shouldn't have dragged her into it."

What did he mean by that? He'd seemed to be living a golden life.

He popped open his door. "Let's order. My treat."

Her mouth watered at the thought of a hazelnut latte, but she shouldn't take advantage of Nash's generosity.

"I brought water."

"You're sure?"

She hesitated before finally giving in, and he motioned for her to follow him.

"We can sit over there." He nodded to the metal tables and chairs surrounded by weeping willows. A brook meandered along the seating area's far side, a natural border between the coffee shop and an old brick church and graveyard. Old-fashioned torches provided light for the tables, but the graveyard was draped in shadows. Not the most picturesque place to relax.

Together, they went inside the shop and got in line. The baristas were efficient, and Nash and Skye walked out with their orders a few minutes later. The calm night air was comfortable against her skin. The crickets' song swelled and waned, competing with the brook's trickle and the distant thrum of traffic. She followed him to a table next to the water and chose to sit with her back to the headstones. She didn't need the morose reminder of Lucy's upcoming funeral.

Removing the lid, she savored the nutty, creamy concoction and pillows of whipped cream. Nash didn't drink his so much as turn the paper sleeve around and around and stare into the shadows.

"What did you mean earlier?" she asked. "About having your own troubles back in high school?"

He chose that moment to take a long sip of his plain black coffee. "Oh, you know, geometry problems and those infernal essays Mrs. Teague liked to assign. And the speeches." He groaned. "Practice did not make perfect."

"You're a pro at deflection, you know that?"

He tipped up his Stetson to scratch behind his ear. "Seems more polite than saying I don't want to talk about it."

"The cowboy code is a thing," she quipped.

"My mama taught me well."

"I remember her," Skye said. "Glory was kind, and she smelled like gardenias."

His smile was tinged with sadness. "She was the best I could've asked for, and I thank God for the years I had with her."

Skye was contemplating his words when a sharp sound hurtled through the night. Nash tackled her, knocking her and her chair to the ground and using his body as a shield.

"Can't reach my gun." Skye grunted beneath him.

Nash shifted his weight. The shot had come from the thick bushes behind the restaurant next door. He grabbed her hand and helped her to her feet. "This way."

Staying low, they splashed through the water, plunging through the willow fronds and into the shadowed graveyard. Any hope he'd misinterpreted the sound was dashed when a bullet smashed into the closest tree trunk, splintering the bark. He pulled Skye behind a large headstone.

Skye peered over the top. "I don't have a clear view of the shooter."

Another bullet streaked toward them, this time embedding into the stone they were hiding behind.

"He's on the move." Skye shifted uneasily. "We have to draw him away from any innocent bystanders."

Nash scanned the rows of graves. "We can leapfrog between that garden shed, those trees and the church."

"Let's do it."

Their sprint toward the shed drew fire. Nash positioned himself so that he was blocking Skye. Anticipating a direct hit, he prayed for God's mercy and protection. He'd just learned he was a father. He was Eden's only remaining parent, and he wasn't eager to leave her an orphan before he even got a chance to know her.

They skidded behind the shed, bullets churning grass and dirt in their wake. Skye spoke into her phone, requesting assistance from local authorities.

Nash kept a weapon on him when he was on the ranch. He'd never felt the need to carry in his hometown or anywhere else.

"They're ten minutes out." She put her phone away. "Ready?"

"Yes, ma'am."

Again, they sprinted into the open, staying low as they made for the cluster of trees in the middle of the field. Their attacker opened fire and the onslaught seemed endless. He was determined to end one or both of them. The reason was lost on Nash, and he didn't have time to ponder it.

He followed Skye into the copse of trees, thankful the trunks were wide enough to provide a barrier of sorts. She peered through the branches, her Glock aimed and ready.

He registered movement near the shed they'd just left.

"There." She fired twice.

The shadowed figure dived behind the weathered building.

"Now's our chance," he urged, taking hold of her arm.

Together, they ran the remaining distance to the darkened brick church and ducked around the far side. Skye continued to the front, scaling the shallow steps to the covered portico.

"You keep watch on this side," she instructed. "I'll cover this one."

Nash agreed. This way, the shooter couldn't ambush them. The church property connected with a brown-and-red warehouse surrounded by ponds. Shifting position, he read the illuminated sign: Russell's Koi and Water Gardens.

Nash's body jolted when Skye abruptly began exchanging fire with the shooter.

She launched off the porch, and Nash joined her.

The water garden business was the natural choice, so they sprinted around the warehouse and entered the landscaped area through an open gate. His boots and her sneakers pounded against the curving stone pathways as they dodged benches, bushes and cement statues. A bullet whizzed past Nash's head, and he instinctively seized Skye around the waist and shouldered through bushes on their right. She gasped and slid out of his grasp, sinking into a koi pond on the other side. He lost his footing, as well, and they landed in waist-deep water.

Spluttering and splashing, she held her gun arm aloft to keep the weapon dry. The water was cold, the algae slimy, and the fish swarming between his legs unsettling. They would make too much noise climbing out, so he grasped Skye's upper arm, put a finger to his lips and guided her back toward the bushes.

Her glare was fully visible, thanks to the accent lighting. She silently went along, but he expected a reprimand from her later. *If* they managed to escape.

She had a limited amount of ammo on her person. The shooter could be shouldering a backpack full of it, for all they knew. He may not care about getting caught, as long as he achieved his objective.

The thought raised goose bumps on Nash's exposed arms and neck.

They huddled close together near the bushes, deliberately sinking deeper into the water to try to hide.

Not far off, a rock skittered. Skye stiffened. Her fierce, determined expression made him feel a little better about not being armed himself. She would take the necessary actions to keep them both safe.

A heavy door slammed in the distance, and a powerful beam of light swept over the gardens. "Who's out there?" a man bellowed. "We're closed for the night."

The sound of fleeing footsteps could be heard. Seconds later, the whir of sirens promised backup.

She started to climb out. "I have to go after him."

"It's too dangerous. Wait for backup."

Brows lowered, forehead creased, she considered him. "Don't you want answers? Someone's trying to kill you."

"Your safety is more important than answers."

"You understand this is connected to the attack at the ranch? Forget the disgruntled-neighbor theory. I think whoever killed Lucy is out to get you, too."

SEVEN

Skye replayed the day's events in her head, trying to figure out where she'd gone wrong. Not informing Chen of their plans? Stopping for coffee? Heeding Nash's request to stay put instead of pursuing the shooter?

She folded the last shirt and tucked it into the dresser drawer with the other pint-sized outfits.

"Why isn't she tired?"

Skye leaned against the dresser. Nash sat on the carpet, his back propped against the side of the bed, his legs crossed at the ankles. He'd showered and changed into fresh jeans and a light blue T-shirt with the Glory Cattle Company logo—named after his late mother. His hair was damp, the longer strands slicked off his face. Eden sat close beside him, babbling and playing with her blocks.

"Maeve did say she had a late nap," she reminded him.

He smoothed her wispy blond locks, and she sucked in her lower lip.

"I'll have to remember that late naps aren't a good idea." He covered a yawn.

The past few days had delivered a series of shocks, including the fact someone wanted him dead.

He lifted his face, and his mesmerizing blue gaze met

hers. "Why didn't Lucy tell me? I can't think of anything I said or did to make her think I wouldn't be there for her and my child."

His transparency nearly knocked Skye off her feet. Of course, the fact he was voicing this question to her meant he was desperate, and she was handy. It didn't mean they were close.

Sliding to the floor, she pulled her knees to her chest and wrapped her arms around her shins. "I think the answer is tied to her murder. We assumed Lucy avoided Tulip because of her history with Maeve."

"Maeve gave Lucy a lot of chances. Lucy stealing from her was the last straw."

Skye disliked discussing her late friend's glaring faults, but they couldn't be ignored.

"Telling you about Eden would've meant ties to Tulip she couldn't avoid. She would've been forced to share custody with you."

Anger chased sadness across his handsome face. "Whatever she was avoiding couldn't have warranted keeping my daughter a secret."

"You have a chance to make up for lost time."

His worry was evident. Besides Hardy, who was an honorary member of the Wilder family, and William, Nash's closest friend, who did he have to lean on during a crisis? He and Remi were close, but she hadn't lived in Mississippi for a while.

Skye was tempted to pinch herself. A week ago, she and Nash were barely on speaking terms. Now she was his live-in protector with a front-row seat to his introduction to fatherhood. She was rooting for him to succeed and concerned about the amount of stress he was under.

"When will you speak with Virgil?"

"Tomorrow." She'd hoped to speak to him tonight when they'd picked up Eden, but Maeve had sent him to the store. "I'll wait until the post-funeral reception."

As was tradition, friends and family would converge at the Ackerman home with enough casseroles to feed the entire town. She hadn't yet shared Tara's revelation with Chen or Hank, preferring to chase that lead herself. Even after tonight's attack, Chen didn't believe Lucy's murderer and the person after Nash were one and the same. He wouldn't even consider it, which was not the way to go about an investigation.

"We should try and get some sleep," she said. "I want to pay Zane Chesterfield a visit before the funeral."

"Why?"

"I have to run down leads. If Zane Chesterfield has other interested buyers for the land you want to buy, maybe one of them wants to get you out of the way."

He coughed out a laugh. "That's not the way we do business in Mississippi, Skye."

"Does that land border anything other than the two ranches?"

"A portion of it links to the state road, but it's not large enough to merit an outsider's interest."

"There's nothing that would make it valuable to anyone other than you and the Chesterfields?"

"Not that I know of."

The doorbell pealed. Eden looked up from her blocks, her eyes wide. "Mama?"

Skye's chest ached. The toddler was old enough to recognize her mom's absence and miss her. It broke her heart.

Frowning, Nash got to his feet, his hand resting on his holster. He'd taken his handgun from a safe in his bedroom when they'd arrived back at the ranch. "Stay with her, will you?"

Skye's instincts were to switch places with him, but this was his property. He was not only armed, he'd trained and served with the US Marines. He could handle himself. He'd proved that tonight at the graveyard.

She listened as he greeted the visitor. As soon as she recognized her friend's voice, she scooped Eden into her arms and ventured into the foyer.

"Honoria? What are you doing here?"

Honoria's brown eyes, set in a round, pleasant face and topped with thick brows, reflected a thousand questions. Her wavy brown hair had been pulled into a side ponytail and secured with a wide red ribbon.

"I've been texting you all day." Her gaze bounced from Eden to Nash.

Skye handed Eden to him. "I'm sorry. Today was hectic." She ventured toward her, tossing a glance over her shoulder. "We'll be in the barn, if you have no objections."

"Keep your eyes and ears open."

Closing the door behind her, Skye took Honoria's elbow and steered her across the yard.

"Why are we in a rush?" Honoria demanded.

"You haven't heard about the target on Nash's back?" Reaching the fence that separated the driveway and yard from the workshop, barn and other outbuildings, she opened the gate and waved her friend through.

"What target? I'm here about your living situation," she huffed. "I can't believe you didn't tell me. I had to hear it from Betsy." Her voice dipped in derision at her coworker's name.

The workshop was attached to what the hands referred to as the sales barn, because it used to host cattle sales.

Adjoined to the sales barn was a small cattle barn used for newborn calves and their mothers. Skye flicked on the lights inside the workshop, locked the door behind her and faced her friend. "I was embarrassed."

Honoria spread her hands. "I could've helped somehow. I still can. I'm sure your landlord hasn't found a new tenant yet."

"Oh, you have piles of money in the bank, do you?"

She arched a thick brow and folded her arms over her chest. "Leo and I have some savings."

Skye braced her hands on Honoria's upper arms. "I love you for that, but I got myself into this mess. I'll get myself out of it."

"When are you going to learn that you can't go it alone your whole life? God put us here for community. To love, support and encourage each other."

Skye dropped her hands. Honoria didn't understand. She'd grown up in a loving, well-adjusted family and married a wonderful man. God had taken away Skye's main support. When He'd taken her dad, He'd essentially taken away her mother, too. And now she couldn't even have a conversation with her sister. She pressed her hands to her eyes and willed herself to focus on the present and not the should've-beens.

"If you didn't want to accept our money, you could've crashed at our place. How did you land at Nash Wilder's?"

Although Honoria had moved to Tulip after high school, she was aware of Skye's history with the elusive rancher.

"It started with Lucy's murder." One of the ranch cats emerged from beneath the workbench and slinked over to wind between her feet. She picked him up and rubbed his soft orange fur. "Her last request was for me to reunite Nash and Eden. I couldn't leave her with him until we got the paternity results, and the investigation is still ongoing. Plus, he doesn't have experience with children, and he has the ranch work…"

Honoria studied her closely. "I thought you despised the man."

Heat rose to her cheeks. "I never said that."

She chuckled. "Not in so many words, maybe."

She'd only *thought* she despised him. Turned out, she'd despised a version of him she'd created in her head over a decade ago.

"My opinion of Nash Wilder isn't important. I've been tasked with protecting him."

"People are worried, especially with Sheriff Hines out of town."

"Chen, Hank and I will do everything in our power to keep the citizens safe."

"Who's going to keep *you* safe?"

Skye's pulse skittered. "Honoria, I do need a favor."

"Anything."

"If something happens to me, will you watch over Dove? Don't let her go back to that other facility, and visit her when you can."

"Oh, sweetie." Honoria wrapped her in a hug, and Skye made herself relax. "I pray for you often, my friend. You can trust Him to work all things together for good."

She fought a wave of tears. If only she could "let go and let God," as the popular saying went. She got so weary of depending on herself. Pulling away, she ducked her head, using her hair as a curtain to hide her face.

"Will you do it, then?"

"You don't have to worry about your sister, Skye. I'll watch out for her."

The tension inside her didn't ebb. Until she'd walked into that dilapidated house and found her old friend on death's door, she hadn't let herself consider that something could happen to her and what that would mean for Dove's future. Now a murderer was on the loose in her hometown, and she was standing between him and his target.

Nash let his rope fly, and it fell over the calf's head. The calf bucked in the morning sunshine. Planting his boots wide in the grass, he held tightly to the rope, feeling the tug through his work gloves. Bella, the high-strung mama cow, inserted her bulk between her baby and Nash. She didn't realize the calf had scours and would die if he didn't get medicine.

"Santi, a little help?"

The older man moved in and tried to hold Bella off.

"Hey, cow." Nash's biceps went taut as the calf bucked again. "Only trying to help."

Between him and Santi, they managed to wrangle the pair close to the truck. While Santi kept the mom at bay, Nash administered antibiotics and then released the calf.

"You've got visitors." Santi hooked a thumb over his shoulder.

Nash tossed the empty syringe into the box on the truck bed. Shifting, he spotted Skye walking hand in hand with Eden. He left Santi in the field and strode toward the barn, his heart in his throat. They were dressed for Lucy's funeral. Skye's black dress and low-heeled shoes looked like they didn't get taken out of the closet often. Her eyes were ringed with liner, and her lips were painted candy-apple red. She'd left her curls to dance in the magnolia-scented breeze. In or out of uniform, Skye Saddler could stop traffic. Something he had no business thinking or noticing.

He gripped the top fence slat. "Is it time to leave already?"

"We have to make a stop first, remember?"

Nash wasn't looking forward to the coming conversation with Zane. When Nash had returned to run the ranch in his father's wake, the local ranchers and farmers had been wary, unsure what to expect from Wes Wilder's son. He'd worked hard to earn their respect and trust. This deal with Zane could go south if he wasn't careful.

"You put her hair in pigtails." He nodded to Eden, who was as pretty as a spring rose in her yellow dress.

Skye smiled. "We discovered she likes yellow and is tender-headed. You'll have to be gentle when brushing her hair."

He wondered if he should start an actual list of all the things he needed to know as Eden's father. "I'll go change."

After a quick word with Santi, Nash returned to the house and found a plate of chocolate-chip waffles waiting for him in the kitchen. Grinning to himself, he wolfed them down standing at the counter.

Lord, I don't understand Your ways. I can't begin to guess why You brought Skye, of all people, into my life at this exact time. I thank You, Jesus, because she's the answer to a prayer I hadn't even uttered. She's making this transition into fatherhood a lot less earth-shattering than it could've been.

Dressed in the suit he'd worn to his father's funeral, he ventured into the sales barn and found the girls doling out treats to the ranch cats.

Skye straightened. "Eden, your daddy's here."

Eden gazed up at him with wide, trusting eyes.

Emotions pinged through him with the speed of a bullet. Wonder. Disbelief. Fear. He couldn't quite grasp that he had a daughter and that now he was responsible for her.

He tried to regain his composure as Skye settled Eden

in her car seat. Skye was perceptive, and she wasn't afraid to press him to reveal his thoughts and feelings.

Thankfully, she didn't notice his mood now. Or maybe she was lost in her own thoughts. Today wasn't going to be a breeze.

Several miles away, he turned off the state road and through the Chesterfield Ranch entrance gate. Zane's herd of Brahman cattle grazed in pastures, lifting their heads as the truck passed by.

"These look different than yours."

He grunted. "They are. Brahmans make great mothers, but they can be feisty."

Nash parked his truck near the brick rancher Zane and his adult son, Bubba, shared. He glanced over at Skye. "Let's keep this friendly, okay?"

Her hands were folded in her lap, her nails short and unpainted. "Why is it so important for you to acquire this land from him?" she asked.

Nash wasn't about to share his true reasons. The fact that he was out to prove something to his deceased father would sound ridiculous to her.

"I want to expand. Can't do that without more acreage."

Nash exited the truck and went to unbuckle Eden. She was a quiet, cautious little thing. Time would tell if this was her natural disposition or not.

His knock went unanswered. Walking around the side of the house, they skirted overgrown azalea bushes and beat a path through the grass toward the weathered barn. They found Zane in the shade of an old gnarly oak, tinkering with an ancient Chevelle.

At their greeting, the burly man straightened, dropped a tool in the dirt at his feet and tipped up his battered hat. "Mornin', Nash. Deputy."

Although in his midfifties, Zane could pass for a man a decade younger. Must be due to good genes, because a rancher's life was hard on a body. He had thick black hair, with only a hint of silver threading through it, and clear gray eyes. His daily work with horses and cattle kept him trim. "Who's that with you?"

"This is Eden. My daughter." He held her higher against his chest, and her blue eyes lifted to his at the mention of her name. His breath caught, and he feared he was going to have an emotional outburst right there in front of his neighbor and Skye.

As if sensing his dilemma, Skye stepped closer and put her palm flat against his back. The weight of her hand through the suit jacket brought another layer of distraction for his brain to process.

"Mr. Chesterfield, I asked Nash to bring me here. You've heard of the trouble on his ranch?"

He slowly nodded, his shoulders tensing.

"Did you also hear someone tried to kill us last night?"

His gaze swerved to Nash. "What happened?"

Nash told him, unconsciously holding Eden tighter.

"Do you know who did it?"

"We're working on it," Skye said. "Have you had any incidents here? Have your employees mentioned seeing or hearing anything unusual in the past few days?"

One hand draped over his belt buckle, he shook his head. "It's been business as usual."

Movement at the barn entrance caught Nash's attention. The man emerging was taller than Zane, but he had the same black hair and burly build. He came to a halt the moment he saw them.

"Would your son be willing to talk to us?" Skye asked.

Zane waved Bubba over. Nash hadn't had much interaction with the younger man. He hadn't been involved in the deal Nash and Zane had struck. For some reason, Bubba gave off hostile vibes.

His face was a blank canvas, but his brown eyes seethed with anger. Skye repeated her questions, and he stated he didn't have any useful information. Nash caught him shooting furtive glances at Eden, something he was going to have to get used to, he supposed, at least until everyone in Tulip had heard the news.

"Mr. Chesterfield, was anyone else interested in buying your property?"

"No, ma'am." Zane cast a sideways glance at Bubba. "I reached out to Nash first, seeing as he's the most obvious first choice. He was interested, so I didn't approach anyone else about it."

"Did you happen to mention the sale to anyone?"

Bubba huffed. "We don't air our laundry."

"If you or your employees think of anything useful, please let me know."

Zane touched the brim of his hat. "We surely will, Deputy."

Back in the truck, Nash blasted the air-conditioning. The men watched their retreat.

Once out of sight, Skye turned her head.

"Has there been trouble between you and Bubba Chesterfield?"

"No. Why?"

"He doesn't like you."

"I've hardly spoken ten words to the man."

She tilted her head, considering him. "Is he unhappy about the sale?"

"No one wants to have to sell off family property."

"Hmm."

"What are you thinking?"

"I'm wondering how unhappy he is that you're benefiting from their misfortune. I'm also wondering if Bubba would try to stop the sale."

"Killing me is a bit extreme."

"Human nature can be extreme and unpredictable."

EIGHT

Skye wished she could melt into the embossed wall-paper on the Ackermans' walls. The funeral attendees had converged at Maeve and Virgil's, and the overflow had spilled into the rear yard. There was an undercurrent of morbid curiosity and a lack of sincere grief that rubbed her the wrong way. Lucy didn't deserve this spectacle.

Her gaze was drawn to the oversized photo in the opposite corner. Flashes of her friend's last moments taunted her. Skye willed away the threatening tears. Later, when she was alone, she'd grieve her friend.

She nursed her sweet tea and contemplated each person in turn. Stationed beside the fireplace, she had an unobstructed view of the living area that flowed into the formal dining space. Maeve was surrounded by her closest friends, most of whom, Skye knew, were from her book club or charitable organizations.

Although Virgil had been at the church, he was nowhere to be seen at the moment. Was he making himself scarce because he had a troubled conscience?

Hank bustled toward her from a side hallway. Her fellow officer patted her shoulder. "How are you holding up?"

"Me? I'm fine. Why do you ask?"

"Your assignment as Nash Wilder's protector." His look could only be described as fatherly. "We both know Chen has an ulterior motive."

She angled toward him. "What would that be?"

"He's threatened by you. You're smarter than him, and he knows it. Doesn't want to be upstaged by a woman if you solve the case and get the credit."

Skye hadn't had a chance to analyze the sergeant's motives. She'd put his behavior down to arrogance. Hank's theory made sense. Indignation surged, and she pushed it down. Anger at Chen wouldn't accomplish anything. The best revenge would be to do exactly what he didn't want her to do.

"He has to be aware of the history between you and Nash," Hank insisted.

"Maybe."

People in Tulip liked to gossip, but her and Nash's high school days were in the past.

"Here's a question," she said. "Why won't he consider a possible link between Lucy's killer and Nash's attacker?"

"Could be he is considering it but doesn't want you to know."

She wondered whether or not to share Tara's tip about Virgil. While she trusted Hank, she wanted to keep this one close for now.

Nash emerged from the kitchen with a plate of food and Eden clinging to his hand. He scanned the room, ultimately locating her and heading in her direction. She ignored the thrill zipping through her. His hair was slicked back from his forehead, showing off his square-jawed, appealing features. He'd removed his tie, and his powder blue dress shirt was open at the neck, revealing tan skin. The navy suit jacket molded to his broad shoulders.

Maeve diverted his attention. She fawned over Eden, boosting her into her arms and welcoming her friends' admiring comments. Nash's mouth tightened slightly, and he continued over to the fireplace to stand next to Skye.

She glanced at his plate. "Is that a typical cowboy diet?"

"This is for Eden…if Maeve ever decides to relinquish her."

"We should take advantage of her distraction and question Virgil."

His blue eyes cut to her. "I haven't seen him since the church."

"Want to help me search for him?"

In answer, he set the plate on the mantel.

She tilted her head toward the nearby hallway. "Let's try the bedrooms first."

They walked past guest bedrooms and a workout room. The last one on the right, the one that had belonged to Lucy, was now an office. The master suite was at the end of the hall and was the only one with a closed door. Her knock went unanswered.

She pivoted, brushing against Nash's hard chest in the process. His strong, calloused hand came up to steady her, curling around her bare upper arm. His face was inches away, and she tumbled into his sea-blue eyes, fascinated by the outer ring of color and long, thick lashes. He didn't seem inclined to release her.

Skye felt as if she were in a midsummer heat wave. Her skin was on fire. Breaking eye contact, she stared at the triangle of tanned skin revealed by his unbuttoned shirt.

"Where would you hide from a house full of mourners?" Her voice sounded breathless to her own ears.

This reaction to Nash was ridiculous in the extreme.

She really needed to join a dating site and actually go out with someone.

His fingers trailed away in a lengthy caress. "The garage?"

Nodding wordlessly, Skye barged ahead, her heels clacking on the hardwood. Outside, she welcomed the fresh air scented with freshly mowed grass and gardenias. They walked along the brick path winding between the house and the mature trees lining the driveway, eventually veering away from the lush yard and approaching the garage's side door. She turned the knob, found it unlocked and entered first.

"Virgil?"

Nash was right behind her as they wound their way between a fishing boat, a car covered with a protective tarp and gleaming vintage lockers.

She tucked a wayward curl behind her ear. "Where to next?"

A light clicked in his eyes. "Follow me."

Outside once again, Skye followed him along a dirt path tucked between the garage and hedges. He turned the corner, stopped and shifted to make room for her. She smelled the cigar odor before noticing the man leaning against the brick and staring at nothing. He looked over at them, lowered the cigar and sighed.

"Hello, Virgil."

"If you're looking for privacy, this is the best spot," he said, his brown gaze shifting between them in dull curiosity.

"We were looking for you, actually," Nash drawled, crossing his arms over his chest.

Taking another drag of the cigar, he pushed off the wall. "I was out of town when Lucy was killed. I don't have any information to share. In case you haven't heard, I wasn't her favorite person."

"You admit you had a strained relationship?" Skye asked.

"Are you eyeing *me* for her murder? Skye Saddler, I'm disappointed. You know me." He bumped his fist against his chest. "You and your sister practically lived here during summer breaks. We took you camping. Took you to the beach. Fed you when your mom used up all her money buying booze."

Skye flinched as shame flooded her. All these years, she'd tried to distance herself from her mother's shadow, tried to prove she was better. Losing her apartment must be a signal to the town that she was as irresponsible as her mother.

Nash edged closer to her, and she took it as a silent show of support. "We spoke to Lucy's roommate, Virgil," he said. "She said Lucy had a problem with you. What kind of problem?"

His face flushed red. "I tried to be a father to her. I came into this marriage thinking we could be a real family, but that girl was wild."

"Wild?" Skye retorted. "That's harsh. Lucy was a dreamer. Sure, sometimes she acted on impulse, but she wasn't rebellious."

Virgil rolled his eyes. "You always had a blind spot where Lucy was concerned."

"It's true she got caught up in her addiction, but she overcame it in the end." Skye tried to regain control of the conversation and her emotions. Not easy when the victim was tied to her past. "I find it curious that Lucy, who didn't share a whole lot of private information with her roommate, saw fit to mention you at all."

"I didn't kill her. I had no reason to. If you're fishing

for a suspect, shift your pole in the direction of Bubba Chesterfield."

"Bubba has no ties to Lucy," Nash scoffed. "Not in the past, and not now."

Why would Virgil point them in his direction? Five years younger than them, Bubba hadn't been at the high school at the same time. He'd had a completely different set of friends.

"What do you know?" she asked.

Nash cast her a disbelieving look, which she ignored.

"Bubba and Lucy became friendly in recent years," Virgil said.

"You know this how?"

"Maeve." He extinguished his cigar in the concrete planter next to the camp chair. "Now, if you're finished interrogating me, I'm going to find my wife."

He stalked around the corner, leaving them in the private area.

"You don't seriously believe him?" Nash demanded. "How would Bubba and Lucy have crossed paths after she moved away?"

"I don't know, but I'm going to find out."

Later that night, after Eden was fast asleep and Skye was occupied with a phone call, Nash retreated to the horse barn. The familiar scents of hay, leather and horseflesh wrapped around him like a hug. It had been an emotionally wrenching day, with highs and lows, regrets and disappointment. Anger seethed at his core. Someone had dared to kill a young mother with an innocent, vulnerable child right outside, and that someone was walking around free. He wanted justice for Lucy, of course, but he also wanted his daughter to be safe.

He greeted each of the horses with an apple, saving

Rico for last. He eased one hip against the stall door and stroked Rico's mane. He was missing time in the saddle these past few days, and it seemed like his trusted sidekick had missed him, too. Ranch operations couldn't be ignored. Neither could his daughter's needs. If not for Skye and Hardy, he wouldn't know which way to turn.

Thank You, Lord, for supplying help when I most need it. Hardy was part of the family, and Nash trusted him to run things. The man was devoted to Glory Cattle Company's success. Skye was someone Nash had known his whole life, but he didn't really *know* her. Still, he trusted her to protect his daughter.

"Well, Rico, I can't put this off any longer," he sighed, pulling his phone from his pocket and calling his sister.

She answered on the third ring, her face appearing on the screen. Her shining eyes and wide smile made him realize how much he missed her.

"Nash! What's happening?"

He was relieved to see she was walking through her apartment and not out with friends or on the job. She worked with the Atlanta police department.

"Are you busy?"

"If you call binge-watching a predictable crime series and eating ice cream busy, then yes, I am." She plopped onto her couch and scooped a hefty mound of ice cream into her mouth.

"I'm glad you're sitting down."

Her mouth full, her pale brows tucked together. "You look like your horse died. Is Rico okay? Is it my horse?"

"The horses are fine." He sucked in a fortifying breath. "There's no easy way to say this, Rem. Lucy and I— Well, it turns out I have a daughter I didn't know about. Her name is Eden, and she's almost three years old."

Remi's jaw hit her chest as her spoon clinked onto the coffee table. "Excuse me?"

"Lucy was murdered a few days ago in Tulip. She had Eden with her." At Remi's gasp, he held up his hand. "She's unharmed. We don't know who did it. Yet." He decided she didn't need to know about the attempts on his life.

"I can't believe this. Nash, you're a father!" Her blue eyes were the size of quarters. "I didn't realize you'd kept in touch with Lucy after high school."

Embarrassment pinched him. Rubbing the back of his neck, he said, "We didn't. She came around shortly after my return." They shouldn't have been together. He'd known God's view on intimacy, but he'd let emotion lead his decision. "You should see her, Rem. She's beautiful. She's quiet, though. Maybe it's the shock of being with strangers in a new place and wondering where her mom has gone."

Remi's expression was one of concern. "I'm in the middle of a case, Nash. I'd be on the first plane out if I could, but I—"

"I get it. Just come when you can."

"I will. I promise." She tilted her head. "Where is she now?"

"Asleep. Skye's with her."

"Skye Saddler?"

"Do you know another Skye?"

"Lucy's best friend. The one who blamed you for Lucy's troubles. That Skye? You don't need her negativity—"

"It's not like that." He shook his head. "She's actually been a huge help."

Her eyes narrowed. "Why her?"

"For starters, she's carrying out her superior's orders."

"I'm sure she loves that."

"She loved Lucy, and she loves Eden."

Remi set the ice cream container on the coffee table and sank against the cushions. "I'm glad to hear it, but I'm worried. You need someone to cheer you on. Encourage you."

"I do?"

"Yes, Nash, you do. I'm your sister. I know exactly what's running through your head."

They were both silent for a beat, the specter of Wes Wilder rising between them.

"Don't let him ruin this for you, Nash. He was wrong about so many things. Before Mom, he was a different person, remember?"

Nash wasn't sure he agreed with that statement. He remembered only the crushing inability to meet his father's expectations.

"Without Mom to soften him, he became harsh and unyielding, especially with you. But that was his problem, not yours. Promise me you'll let go of the past."

He couldn't make that promise. He wasn't sure he could ever separate his identity from the one his father had pushed onto him.

"I can promise you that I won't make the same mistakes with Eden that Wes made with us."

He would love and support his daughter, no matter what. And he'd do anything to keep her safe.

NINE

The mattress dipped, and a small hand patted Skye's head. "Waffle?"

Her eyes popped open. She was greeted with the sight of Eden sitting on her knees, her hair sweetly mussed and a pillow crease in her cheek. She stroked Skye's curls.

"Waffle?"

Skye's lips curved in a wide smile, and the remnants of sleep dissipated. "You want a waffle?"

Eden sucked on her lower lip as she reached up to tangle her fingers in her own hair.

Skye pushed the sheets aside and put her feet on the floor. "What kind? I saw strawberries in the freezer. Do you want strawberry? Or I could fry up some bacon and put it and some cheese in the waffle."

Eden followed Skye into the bathroom, where they quickly washed up. Skye put on a soft, mint-green shirt and a pair of jean shorts, then slipped her sandals on. She ran her fingers through her hair and applied gloss.

She held out her hand. "Ready?"

Eden slipped her hand into Skye's. Skye found herself wondering what it would be like to have a daughter. She'd been cheated out of a close, loving relationship with her own mother.

In the hallway, the rich scent of coffee wrapped around her. The sound of a woman's lilting voice, followed by Nash's low response, stopped her in her tracks.

Had Remi made an unannounced visit? Unlikely, considering Nash had told Skye last night about their phone conversation and that Remi was busy with work.

She and Eden entered the living area. Nash stood on the other side of the kitchen bar, holding his favorite mug. He was focused on the young woman propped against the counter near the sink.

"Good morning."

At Skye's greeting, Nash straightened and set down his mug. "There you two are. Skye, I'd like to introduce you to someone."

The petite young woman had a cap of shining blond hair and lively brown eyes set in a cute, elfin face. She regarded them with unveiled curiosity.

"This is Grace Thompson. She's taking over for Willie Jo and will be looking after the vegetable garden and running the ranch farm store."

"Nice to meet you." Skye hoped her voice didn't sound strangled. She prayed the green-eyed monster welling up in her wasn't obvious. Seeing Nash in a cozy, Saturday-morning conversation with a perky stranger made her unhappy and suspicious. "Willie Jo is on maternity leave, I gather?"

"That's right," Nash confirmed. "She'll be out for the season. Remi really came through for me by putting me in touch with Grace."

Grace beamed at him. "I'm grateful for the work. Remi used to talk about this place and how beautiful it was. Now that I've seen it for myself, I understand the appeal."

"How do you know Remi?" Skye rested a hand on a bar stool.

"College roommates. My folks live in the next town over, in Farmdale."

"I was telling Remi a few weeks ago that I needed to hire someone," Nash said, "and she recommended Grace."

"It's nice that you stayed in touch with Remi," Skye said.

Instead of offering more information, Grace gestured to Eden. "Is this your daughter, Nash?"

There was barely a moment of hesitation before he nodded and smiled, a sign he was getting used to the idea. He walked around to their side of the bar, allowing Skye a glimpse of his holster belt and sidearm.

He easily scooped Eden into his arms. "Eden, this is Grace. She's going to be working on the ranch." He looked at Skye. "We were about to tour the greenhouse and store."

There was a question in his voice and gaze. Was he wondering if she wanted to tag along?

"Eden and I are going to make breakfast."

His eyes twinkled. "Quiche?"

She mock scowled. "This isn't Lulu's Tearoom."

"Breakfast casserole?"

"I'd like to eat in the next fifteen minutes."

He tapped his chin. "Scrambled eggs."

"Those can be on the menu, if you like."

Skye noticed Grace intensely watching their exchange, and her good humor faded. Did Grace think Skye was flirting with him? Skye reminded herself she wasn't on his payroll. Wasn't his daughter's nanny, either. She was here in an official capacity.

After Nash and Grace left the house, she poured a generous cup of coffee for herself and milk for Eden. She gathered her ingredients and began cooking while Eden sat on the tiled floor and played with her toys.

The house smelled like a diner by the time Nash returned.

"Did Grace leave?" Skye asked, setting the platter of waffles, eggs and bacon on the table. "There's plenty."

After laying his Stetson on a bar stool, he washed his hands in the kitchen sink. "I asked her to join us, but she had errands to run. Tomorrow is her first day."

Eden climbed onto a chair, her sippy cup in one hand. Nash retrieved silverware and napkins and placed them on the table. He tousled Eden's hair and smiled down at her. "Hungry?"

She pointed at the platter. "Waffle."

His eyebrows shot to his hairline and his wide eyes found Skye's.

"I got sidetracked and forgot to tell you. She woke me up and asked for one."

He made a sound between a grunt and a laugh. "Imagine that. One of her first words since coming here is not *Daddy* but *waffle*. Thanks, Skye."

Carrying her mug to the table and claiming a chair, she couldn't hold back a grin. "At least you won't forget it."

He settled across from her, his gaze growing intense. "There's no danger of that. I really appreciate everything you've done for us."

Flustered, she snagged a waffle and poured a generous helping of syrup on top. "Does Grace know what's been going on?"

He inhaled deeply and began cutting a waffle into tiny pieces. "I was up-front with her. I also told her the new security cameras and signs aren't guaranteed to ward off trouble. Neither is parking your cruiser at the entrance. She said her daddy taught her about firearms from a young age, and she's not afraid to use them."

Skye understood that Nash couldn't shut down the cattle company or stop ranch operations indefinitely. Growing and selling produce to the locals generated income.

He handed Eden a small fork and scooped a hefty portion of eggs onto his plate, along with two waffles. "If there's any more trouble on the property, I'll close the store and have her stick to local farmers' markets." He forked a generous bite of the waffle and examined it. "No fruit today?"

"We went the savory route."

"Ever think about opening a waffle truck?"

"You're the enterprising one, not me. Speaking of business... I'm going to seek out Bubba today. I understand if you'd rather not be included in that conversation."

His features tightened. "I want to be there. I'm interested in seeing his reaction."

"You think Virgil tossed us a bone to get the spotlight off himself?"

"I'm undecided."

"Bubba and Lucy as a couple doesn't make sense to me, but who knows what Lucy's mindset was in recent years. She chose to keep you from your daughter, after all." Skye felt compassion for him now that she'd spent time with him and learned his side of the story. "Maybe Bubba's hostility has nothing to do with the land sale. Let's say he was involved with Lucy. Everyone knows about your romantic history with her, but what if he recently learned that you're the father of her child? That could inspire some serious jealousy and competition."

"I suppose it's possible. Would he kill her in a jealous rage, though? It's not like she'd reached out to me."

"Maybe she planned to reveal the truth, and he felt threatened."

Her phone buzzed, and she glanced at the screen. "It's

Hank." She skimmed the terse text and pushed back her chair. "I have to go. There's a wreck out on the highway."

His brows connected as he glanced at Eden.

"I shouldn't be gone long," she added.

"You're doing your job, Skye. Don't worry about us. We'll figure it out. I have to, don't I? You won't be here forever."

He was right. Her personal life was in a holding pattern. As soon as the suspect was apprehended, she'd be on her own again. She didn't want to examine why that thought wasn't appealing.

Nash leaned against the stall with Eden in his arms as she stroked Rico's face. He'd spent the morning introducing her to the ranch animals, including pigs, dogs, cattle, horses and a few unsociable cats, but she'd wanted to come back out to the barn. She seemed to like the horses best, a true sign of a future cowgirl. The wonder and pride mingling inside him was completely new, as was the overwhelming drive to protect her.

After lunch, he'd gotten comfortable in the recliner with her, found a program for young children, and they'd both fallen asleep. He couldn't recall the last time he'd taken a nap.

"What's the plan, boss?"

Hardy, Santi and Dax had congregated in the horse barn this afternoon, taking advantage of the cooler air and shade. He looked each one in the eye.

"I don't have one yet. I have to figure out a care plan for Eden." CPS had insisted on it. His choices were either put her in day care or hire a sitter who'd come to the ranch. He preferred to keep her close. "You three have done a fine job of filling in the gaps for me, and I want you to know I appreciate it."

One booted foot propped against an empty cooler, Dax lifted his hat and shoved his fingers through his sweat-dampened hair. "How long will the deputy be hanging around?"

"I can't say."

Hardy arched a brow, his gaze assessing. Nash tried not to squirm. Could he tell Nash dreaded the day Skye left the ranch for good? Not for personal reasons, of course. She was so good with Eden.

Lord, how curious that the woman I never would've chosen during this time of crisis is the very one I needed.

Santi spit a stream of tobacco juice into an empty bottle. "Do the police have any leads?"

"I don't know much more than anyone else." He couldn't share that Virgil was a suspect, and that the police would potentially consider Bubba, too.

Nash couldn't imagine either man capable of murder. For selfish reasons, he hoped Bubba wasn't involved. This land deal was important.

He heard the slam of a car door and went to greet Skye, who'd texted she was on her way.

He called out to her. "How bad was the accident?"

She was in her uniform, her hair tucked into a tight coil at the nape of her neck. Her green eyes swirled with sadness. "Five-car pileup. Two members of the same family were killed." Reaching over, she cupped Eden's cheek and smiled. "How are you, sweet girl? Enjoying time with your daddy?"

Eden lurched forward and Skye caught her in her arms, her expression tender.

Nash stepped back, fighting the urge to hug away her cares. He imagined dealing with tragedies like that was tougher for Skye, considering she'd experienced one herself.

Her gaze shifting beyond his shoulder, she greeted the men. They mumbled and scattered.

"Are you too tired to go furniture shopping? The sooner I get Eden's room set up, the sooner she'll feel at home."

"I'm fine with that. I'll go get changed."

When Nash attempted to take Eden, she tightened her grip on Skye.

"It's all right. I'll take her inside with me."

Her smile looked motherly and Nash wasn't sure how he felt about it. Eden had already lost her mother. Now she was becoming attached to Skye, who was only in their lives temporarily.

There was nothing he could do about it. She was on the ranch for the duration of this case. He kicked at a bucket, wincing when it whacked against the wall. This whole thing was a sticky mess.

Had Lucy understood the scope of her decision not to include him in Eden's life? That she wasn't hurting just him?

Half an hour later, they cruised down Main Street and parked in the diagonal slot in front of Cox's Furniture. Sandwiched between a bank and a fifties-themed café, the shop was housed in a former bakery. The sidewalks were busy with weekend shoppers. Beautiful flowers winked from cement planters, and ivy crept up the brick walls. The place he'd grown up in, the town he loved, had lost its innocence, and he hated that. Although both he and Skye were armed and trained to handle trouble, he couldn't help but feel exposed.

"Let's make this quick," he muttered.

He studied each person in the vicinity, trying to assess potential danger. His military training was resurfacing, something he never thought would happen in Tulip.

Relaxing music played inside the store. He counted less than a dozen occupants on the first floor. He couldn't see upstairs.

His boots clomped against the honeyed planks. Eden walked between them, holding each of their hands. They entered the children's section of bunk beds, cribs, dressers and all sorts of accessories. He stopped in the middle of the brightly colored rug, unsure where to even begin.

"Priority number one is a bed," Skye said. "They have three toddler-sized beds."

Soon, a salesclerk joined them. She took note of their choices and promised to arrange a next-day delivery. As they were paying, Nash felt someone's hand come down hard on his shoulder. He spun, his fingers reaching for his weapon.

"I thought that was you, Nash. What are you doing here?"

He relaxed, the breath whooshing out of him. "William. You startled me."

His good friend from high school looked like a lumberjack with his long, full beard, plaid shirt and hefty boots. He noticed Nash was armed, and his grin faded.

"Sorry. I forgot for a moment what's been going on." He glanced at Eden and Skye. "Teresa and I don't have any guests booked this weekend, so we came in for a new couch."

"We're here for Eden. She came with clothes, toys and a playpen."

Concern filtered through William's eyes as his wife, Teresa, sauntered up with a smile. "Nash, she's adorable."

"Why don't you all have supper at our place?" William said, glancing at his wife for confirmation. "I have burgers ready for the grill."

"Say yes," Teresa tacked on. "It's been ages since we've entertained anyone other than paying guests."

"She made strawberry shortcake," William added.

Nash looked at Skye. "Teresa makes the best strawberry shortcake around."

"I can't pass that up," she said, lips curving.

"Good. It's settled," William said. "Are you all done here?"

Nash nodded. "What about your couch?"

Teresa waved away his question. "We'll come back Monday morning. William was just saying it's been too long since you two hung out."

At the bed-and-breakfast, Teresa descended the stairs ahead of Skye. "That completes the tour."

"You've done wonders with the place." Skye trailed behind her. "Thanks for showing me around. I haven't been in here since I was a child."

The Victorian house had been many things over the years. Located downtown, one street over from Cox's Furniture, it had sat empty for over a decade and fallen into disrepair. William and Teresa had purchased it several years ago, completed extensive renovations and opened it to guests. Their hard work had benefited Tulip's main business hub.

Her hostess paused at the bottom. The men could be heard conversing in the kitchen as they cleaned the dishes. Eden was in the living room attempting to play with the cat.

"I'm happy we were able to do this." Teresa's brow creased beneath her fringy bangs. "It's been good to visit with Nash. He seems to be doing okay."

"He's holding his own."

"Nash is strong. He's had to be, what with losing his

mom at a young age and being raised by Wes." She grimaced. "A shame Remi doesn't still live here. He tends to shoulder things alone, but he will accept help from her."

"I didn't realize there were issues with his dad."

"You know Nash. He keeps things close to the vest." She tucked a lock of her short brown hair behind her ear, untangling her gold earring in the process. "I doubt even Lucy knew how Wes treated his son."

Skye's mind whirled, trying to remember if Nash had sported unexplained bruises or broken bones. "He hurt him?"

"Physically? No. He messed with his head, though. You know what God's Word says about building someone up? Wes did the opposite, from what my husband tells me. Living beneath the weight of a parent's constant disappointment must be a terrible burden. Joining the military was the best thing he could've done."

Skye followed Teresa into the kitchen, stunned speechless. She was sure her astonishment showed on her face because Nash tilted his head and narrowed his eyes when he saw her.

He'd mentioned trouble in high school. When she'd questioned him at the coffee shop, he'd shrugged it off as typical teenage problems.

"We should get going," Nash said. "Eden will probably need a bath before bed."

William pulled Nash in for a half hug and hearty smack on the back. "You need anything, call me."

Skye thanked the couple for their hospitality. While she had dedicated her life to the citizens of this town, she didn't often get to interact with them in a nonofficial way. Nash's friends had made her feel like part of the group. The visit had been a welcome distraction from the tension and roller-coaster emotions of recent days.

Nash was the first one out of the house. "Let me take a look around before you bring Eden to the truck."

Skye was about to insist they switch places when the sound of a gunshot shattered the calm. Eyes wide, he looked down at the blood soaking through his jeans. Then his knees buckled, and he sank to the ground.

TEN

Skye and William converged on Nash. They dragged him into the foyer and propped him against the wall. His face was ashen. With one hand pressed against the wound in his thigh, he attempted to scan the parking area through the glass storm door.

"Get Eden out of here," he grunted, pain punctuating each word.

William called out to his wife, who was already carrying the crying girl upstairs. He then looked at Skye. "I've got this."

He expected her to pursue the shooter. That was her job. But Nash's face was locked in agony, and his blood loss appeared to be significant. Her personal feelings collided with her professional responsibility, ripping her apart. It shocked. Scared her. He was no longer the Nash from her past, her friend's sorry excuse for a boyfriend and the object of her disdain. He was a grown man with strengths and weaknesses, quirks and foibles. He was someone she was starting to care for.

William pulled out his phone and dialed 9-1-1.

"Skye." Nash stared hard at her. "I'll be fine."

With a terse nod, she withdrew her Glock and eased through the door, forcing herself to focus on the task at hand. She advanced into the parking area, using Nash's truck for cover as she surveyed her surroundings. Fox Street ran between the bed-and-breakfast and the back lot shared by the furniture store, restaurant and bank. The restaurant had patio seating, and Skye observed the manager urging a couple to come inside.

She heard the sound of a garbage can being overturned on the other side of the hedges, followed by the thrum of retreating footsteps. She gave chase down the sidewalk, veering right at the next intersection, plunging into the honeysuckle bushes and emerging in front of the chocolate shop. A flash of black lured her around the next corner. She blasted past the wrought-iron fence surrounding the outdoor seating area and battled through dense vegetation. By the time she emerged onto the street, the shooter was nowhere in sight. She waited there for a time, hoping he'd reveal himself, but she eventually accepted he'd slipped through her fingers…again.

Lungs heaving and a stitch in her side, she jogged back to the bed-and-breakfast. An ambulance was parked near the house, engine humming, rear doors thrown open. Paramedics emerged from the house.

Dashing over, she caught up to them before they loaded Nash inside.

His jaw was rock-hard. "He got away?"

"Yes." The admission pained her.

"They're insisting I go to the hospital. They can just as easily treat me here. Reason with them, Skye."

She glanced at the female paramedic, who firmly shook her head.

Skye squeezed his arm. "I trust their judgment, and so should you."

William bustled over. "Go with him, Skye. Teresa and I will take care of Eden."

"I don't need a babysitter," Nash groused while being boosted into the ambulance.

Skye held out her hand. "Give me your truck keys. I'll meet you at the hospital."

Nash wore a disgruntled expression as he handed them over.

"I'll be right behind you," she said.

He fisted his hands and closed his eyes.

Skye bit her lip. She had failed him. If the shooter's aim had been better, she could be dealing with a second murder victim. Some protector she was turning out to be.

Nash forced his legs over the side of the hospital bed, gritting his teeth and trying to push through the pain. The nurses had offered him an intravenous pain reliever, but he'd opted for a localized numbing injection and over-the-counter meds. Keeping a clear head was crucial. Look what one moment of distraction had led to…and it could've been much, much worse. He thanked God for His protection.

This temporary room in the ER department had a square glass insert in the door, and through it, he had a good view of Skye and Sergeant Chen. Judging by her crossed arms, compressed lips and knotted brow, the conversation wasn't pleasant. Nash dismissed the surprising urge to go out there and defend her to her superior. Skye Saddler could take care of herself.

Knowing that didn't mean he didn't worry about her. He had been tempted to try to stop her from pursuing the shooter. Watching her race into the night alone had been difficult. Surprising, considering a mere week ago his concern would've been impersonal. Now her safety—and Eden's—had climbed to the top of his priority list.

His preconceived notions about Skye were being

eroded by the day. Her interactions with his daughter had shown him a gentle, loving side that was both unexpected and powerful. He hadn't thought her capable of such tenderness. Made him wonder what other revelations he might discover.

The door opened, and Skye stalked in. He could almost see steam coming out of her ears. She closed the door behind her with a restrained click and raised her brows at him.

"What are you doing?" she asked.

"Going home." He pushed to his feet and gasped at the lightning-hot bolts arcing through his upper leg.

Skye dashed over to steady him, bracing her hands on his biceps. His hands navigated to her waist, and he found himself staring down into her upturned face and losing himself in her green eyes. Her curls were disheveled and there was a streak of dirt on her cheek. She robbed him of breath.

"Where are my clothes?" His voice was rusty.

"The nurses have your things. They haven't discharged you, have they?"

"Not in so many words."

"Nash, you were shot tonight."

"You heard the doctor. It's not that serious."

"A bullet passed through your body." Her expression reflected more than a professional concern for him, and his heart flipped over.

"It didn't leave any lasting damage, and I avoided surgery. The Lord was gracious." He was more than a little overwhelmed by God's kindness. "Eden needs me, and I have cattle to tend to."

"Eden is in good hands. So is the ranch. Hardy can run that place with one hand tied behind his back." She slid her hands to his chest, sucked in a sharp breath and quickly stepped back. "Get back into bed and rest. You are capable of that, right?"

He sank onto the mattress. "I'll rest when this guy is behind bars. What was Chen saying to you?"

Skye opened a can of soda, poured half the contents into a paper cup and handed it to him. Then she chugged the rest and lobbed it into the trash can.

"He's unhappy with my performance."

"I assume he thinks he could've done better?"

"He's right. I've let the perp slip through my fingers more than once."

"And yet he's not willing to put his life on hold for me and Eden. If he was, he would've taken us on himself. You're the one risking your safety, not him."

Her expression clouded. Before she could respond, her phone trilled. She put it to her ear. "What's up?"

Nash could make out a male voice, but he couldn't hear what was being said. Her brows tugged together as her gaze glanced off him. "I see. Thanks for letting me know. I'll come straightaway." She hung up. "That was William. Eden is upset. They've tried everything they can think of, but nothing is working. I'll pick her up and take her to the ranch."

He could imagine how frightened she must be. Although he hadn't been a father for very long, his need to protect Eden felt as natural as breathing. "I'm coming with you."

Skye didn't try to talk him out of it. "Let me find your nurse first. Get some wound-care instructions, at least. I'm sure you'll have a prescription or two."

Nash waited impatiently for her to return. After receiving a detailed review of his discharge papers, he changed into his shirt and a pair of scrubs pants, since his jeans had to be chucked. Skye insisted on driving them to the bed-and-breakfast.

"Sit tight." She got out and met Teresa and William near the porch.

In the glare of the headlights, he could see Eden's little chest hitching with the remnants of her sobs. Her face was splotchy. She looked miserable, and Nash's heart dissolved into a pool of helplessness.

How, Lord? How is it that I already love her? I barely know my child, but I'm ready to slay dragons for her.

As soon as she spied Nash, she reached for him. He opened the door and got out, unhappy with his body's frailty. Now wasn't the time for weakness. Aware of the potential of lurking danger, he climbed into the back seat while Skye buckled Eden in next to him. He spoke soothing words, smoothing her hair and bringing his forehead to hers. Although she wanted to be held, this closeness would have to suffice.

Skye's manner was subdued during the ride home. Once there, she carried Eden inside, flipping on lights and ordering him to bed as if she owned the place. Eyes droopy, Eden laid her head on Skye's shoulder.

"I'll help you get her down first," he said.

Skye assessed him for long moments, probably debating whether or not it was worth the energy to argue. Shrugging, she went into the bathroom and turned on the tub faucet. He followed, gathering a towel, soap and bath toys. Halfway through the bedtime routine, Nash couldn't fight the fatigue or the pain any longer. He retreated to Eden's bedroom and sprawled on the bed. He woke up hours later, disoriented and groggy.

Eden's breath puffed across his face. He turned his head. Her small, warm form was tucked close beside him. He checked his watch…half past three. His stomach growled and his thigh throbbed. Careful not to disturb her, he eased out of the room and trod lightly down the hallway. He'd fallen asleep with his boots on. Skye must've decided to leave him as he was.

The night-light Skye had insisted he purchase cast the living room in a muted glow. Skye was fast asleep on the couch, curved on her side, her hands tucked near her face. Her dark curls were splayed over the pillow, and stray strands tickled her cheek. Her worries must've followed her into her sleep, because she looked far from peaceful. He didn't feel free to smooth her brow or caress her cheek. Nash didn't know what was troubling her aside from this case, and he wanted to. He wanted her to confide in him. To trust him. To respect and even like him. He'd told himself all those years ago that her poor opinion of him didn't matter, and maybe it hadn't. It did now.

He began to pray for her, for the problems that plagued her. He prayed for himself, as well, because he was starting to want more than her friendship. Skye almost certainly didn't share those feelings. Besides, a successful relationship required openness and trust—and he wasn't sure he would ever be capable of that.

ELEVEN

Skye battled rising indignation as she went in search of Nash early Sunday morning with Eden riding on her hip. She reviewed what she would say to him if she found him in the saddle or doing chores. Leaving the hospital before it was wise was one thing. Refusing to rest and take proper care of his wound was another. She wouldn't tolerate it, even if that meant handcuffing him to the couch.

She followed voices to the area between the sales barn and paddocks and saw Santi and Dax drive away in the ranch truck with one of the trailers hitched to it. Hardy and Nash stood near the cattle pens.

Hardy noticed her first. He inclined his head in greeting and nudged Nash, who tipped up his Stetson and waved.

"Morning, ladies."

Eden squirmed down, made a beeline to Nash and leaned into his side. Skye's heart melted anew. Hadn't taken long for the little girl to become attached.

Watch out that you don't follow suit—to either one of them. You have no future with the Wilder family.

In her mind, Nash would always belong to Lucy. He would always be the wealthy rancher out of reach for the poor daughter of the town drunk. Besides, how could she contemplate a relationship when it was her fault her little sister required twenty-four-hour care?

"Nash. Hardy." She lifted the bag. "I brought breakfast. There's plenty for everyone."

Nash's brows quirked. "Mighty thoughtful of you. What kind of waffles did you make us?"

"They're egg-and-sausage burritos. Even I occasionally need a break from waffles."

Nash handed one of the foil packages to Hardy before unwrapping one for himself. Hardy took a bite and gave her a thumbs-up.

"Thanks, Skye. Nash never cooks us breakfast."

"You're a better cook than me, Hardy," Nash protested between bites. He peered into the bag. "Do I have to save the rest? Santi and Dax will never know."

She couldn't stop her smile, even though she was still perturbed that he wasn't inside resting. "There's enough for everyone to have two."

"Only two? I'm injured, so I should have extra."

The reminder put a scowl on Hardy's face. Her own moment of lightheartedness faded. If the bullet had severed a major artery… If it had damaged bone…

"Don't worry," he said as though reading her thoughts. "I'm fine."

"You won't be if you don't take care of yourself." She planted her hands on her hips and glared at him. "You'll have me to answer to."

Hardy ducked his head. "I need more coffee."

When he'd gone, she said, "Why are you out here, anyway? The wound isn't going to heal properly if you insist on playing cowboy."

"Playing?" He paused in unwrapping another burrito. "I *am* a cowboy. I have people and animals depending on me. Put your mind at ease, woman. I'm not planning on mucking stalls or manhandling cows. I got a call from a buyer wanting a hundred head of cattle, so I came out to speak to the men. Santi and Dax are off to the stockyards to weigh the empty trailer. The cattle will need sorting before being weighed and delivered."

The last of her indignation evaporated, only to be replaced by a spark of annoyance when Grace rounded the workshop calling for Nash. At least, she hoped it was annoyance. What did she care if a young, beautiful, single woman worked day after day right under Nash's nose?

"Nash! I heard you got shot!" Not acknowledging Skye in any way, Grace strode up to him and laid a hand on his arm. "Are you all right?"

"I expect to make a full recovery."

Skye studied the young woman. Granted, news like this traveled fast, but Grace lived in the next town over. "How did you hear about it?"

"Rachel, one of the responding paramedics, lives next door to me, and she knows I'm working here. Is there anything I can do for you, Nash? Anything at all?"

The way Nash smiled at Grace made Skye's blood simmer.

"Not a single thing, but I appreciate the offer."

"Well, I wanted to tell you the strawberries are going to yield a nice crop. The peppers are struggling, though."

She started to explain her thoughts on how best to remedy the situation. Skye watched Nash's face closely. The thought that he and Grace made an attractive pair soured her mood further.

Her phone rang. At the number flashing on the screen, her pulse skyrocketed. "I have to take this."

Hurriedly walking farther down the fence line, she answered the call and listened as a nurse at Dove's care facility requested her presence.

"I'm on my way," she stated.

"What's wrong?"

Skye jerked, surprised to find Nash at her elbow. He held Eden in his arms. "I have to go to my sister. I typically visit on Sunday afternoons. I wasn't going to go today at all, but she apparently had a bad night. It happens sometimes. My presence calms her down."

"We're coming with you."

"No, Nash. Your leg—"

"I'll be resting in the truck while you drive."

Skye didn't come out and say it, but she was glad not to have to go alone.

Located an hour south of Tulip, the facility was a complex of brick buildings with shingled roofs, sparkling windows and blue shutters. The neat green lawns had walking paths winding around colorful flower beds, cement fountains and benches.

"Has Dove been here since the beginning?"

Skye's jaw was brittle as she switched off the engine and handed him the keys. "I had her transferred here two years ago."

"Is this the closest facility you could find?"

"It's the best in this part of Mississippi."

Gentle sunshine blanketed them, and birds chorused from the dogwoods as they walked along the sidewalk. The lobby was bright and welcoming. When they encountered a nurses' hub, one of them greeted Skye by name.

Skye introduced him. "Laura, this is my friend Nash Wilder. Is it okay if we go on in?"

"I'm glad you're here. There's been no change since I called you." The gray-haired lady led them down a hall. Halfway down, she pushed open a door and gestured inside. "I'll be around if you need me."

"Thanks, Laura."

Low moans wafted out into the hallway, and Skye squared her shoulders before entering. Nash followed in her wake, only to halt just inside the door. He hadn't set eyes on Dove Saddler in over a decade. The last time he'd seen her, she'd been a high school sophomore—shy, sweet-natured and full of life. Seeing her lying helpless and vulnerable, seemingly unaware of her surroundings, temporarily robbed him of thought.

Skye got into bed and wrapped her arm around her little sister, speaking softly into her ear.

Nash's throat was so dry he could hardly swallow. Feeling like an intruder, he turned on his heel and left, ultimately finding his way to a sitting area with toys and books for Eden. She scurried over to the corner to explore, and Nash stared unseeing out the window.

He hadn't been in Tulip when the accident happened. He'd been in boot camp and too focused on surviving Parris Island's drill instructors to spare much thought for the Saddler sisters' tragedy. He hadn't gone to Anita Saddler's funeral. Hadn't been around to hear the locals' gossip. Hadn't seen how Skye had had to navigate life as her sister's guardian.

Skye didn't have extended family in Tulip, nor a large network of close friends. Had she carried this burden alone all these years?

His thoughts continued to spin until Eden lost interest in the toys. Nash decided taking her to the enclosed courtyard would be a welcome distraction. After telling Laura where Skye could find them, they exited through the double glass doors and made their way to a bubbling cement fountain. He sank onto a bench while Eden investigated the fountain.

Skye emerged not long after. Spotting them, she slowly

followed the stone path, her posture wilted and her gaze downcast. She dropped beside him on the bench, straightening her blouse and tugging on the hem of her white shorts.

He propped his arm on the back of the bench. "Is she better now?"

She inhaled deeply and nodded. "Took longer than usual."

"I wasn't sure if you wanted me to stay."

She lifted her gaze to his face, and the sun made her eyes appear translucent. "Your presence is enough."

"I wasn't around at the time of the accident. I only heard bits and pieces. I'd like to know the real story, if it's not too difficult to talk about."

She tucked her hair behind her ear and watched Eden drop pebbles into the fountain. "Dove had gotten a part-time job at Jerry's Ice Cream Treats. It was her first shift, and I volunteered to drive her so she wouldn't have to ride her bike. That job was a big deal, you know? She was so shy, but she needed to make money. My earnings weren't enough to cover the electricity and the groceries. She worked up her courage and approached the owner, who agreed to give her a chance."

Her lips curved in a fleeting, tremulous smile. "She was a mess that day. She was so excited and nervous. Although I wished she didn't have to work, I also thought it would be a good experience for her. An opportunity to boost her confidence."

Skye sounded more like a mother figure than a sister. Based on what he knew of their mom, he guessed Skye had been thrust into the caretaker role at a young age.

Her smile faded. "My mom came home right before we left, and I could smell alcohol on her breath. She'd finished an afternoon shift at the café, so she shouldn't have had a drink already. But she'd stopped by a friend's house." She toyed with the top button on her blouse. "She insisted on driving Dove. We argued. Badly. Dove was the peacemaker, and she said it was all right."

"Surely you don't hold yourself responsible for Anita's actions?"

"I never should've let her get in that car. The thing is, I was used to her drinking. I could tell when she was buzzed and when she was truly out of it. That day, she wasn't out of control, you know? She wasn't slurring her words or tripping over her own feet."

His gut churned. "You never should've been put in that position, Skye. She was the adult. The parent. She was supposed to be the responsible one."

"Well, she wasn't. She worked enough to keep the landlord from breathing down our necks, most of the time, but I made sure Dove ate regular meals, did her homework and had clean clothes to wear."

Nash couldn't help comparing Anita to his own mom. Glory Wilder had been a wonderful mother. She'd made sure their basic needs were met, but she'd also lavished them with love and affection.

Skye was still watching out for her younger sister. "Have you been overseeing Dove's care on your own?"

"I'm all she has." She gripped her knees. "I'll do right by her, whatever it takes."

"This seems like a good place."

"I have no complaints. Unlike the last place."

"There was a problem?"

"It was fine in the beginning. My mom didn't have private insurance, which meant I didn't have a choice which facility Dove went to. Conditions eventually began to deteriorate. I started noticing instances of neglect, and not just with my sister. My complaints to the administrator and insurance people fell on deaf ears. When a case of abuse against a young woman my sister's age came to light, I was horrified. I couldn't let her stay there."

Skye's eviction finally made sense. "Insurance doesn't cover everything here, does it?"

She shook her head, tears trembling on the edges of her dark lashes. She twisted her fingers together. "I can't let her go back to that place. I don't care what I have to do..."

Dove's care was the reason for Skye's money problems. The townspeople probably thought Skye was irresponsible, like her mom, yet she hadn't defended herself.

"What are you going to do once this is all over? You have to take care of your needs, too, Skye."

"I'll figure something out."

She was strong and resilient, but everyone needed a boost sometimes. Would she accept help? From him? That was something he had to ponder. He rested his palm against her upper back and felt her trembling. A tear slipped free to drip off her chin.

"Oh, Skye."

He pressed her closer, and she didn't resist. She came willingly, angling into his side and burying her face against his chest. Her hot tears seeped through his shirt, and a lump balled in the base of his throat, preventing him from speaking. What could he say, anyway? He wasn't good with feelings or words.

Nash sat silently stroking her back. When his fingers found their way into her hair, he closed his eyes against the rush of sensations. This was about comforting her, he reminded himself. Providing a safe place to vent. But she smelled like the best of spring. Her hair was incredibly soft and silky. Having her close felt nice.

Beneath those sensations was a voice screaming at him that this was Skye Saddler, his biggest, loudest detractor. He watched as Eden grabbed a flower and fistful of mulch and dumped them onto Skye's lap. Skye straightened and wiped her cheeks, uncaring that her shorts were now dirty.

"Thank you, sweetheart." She picked up the flower and sniffed it. "Smells nice."

Eden grinned and returned to the flower bed.

"Sorry about that," Skye muttered, keeping her face averted. "I didn't mean to make you uncomfortable."

He shifted forward, took her chin in his hand and gently turned her face to his. The tip of her nose was pink. Her eyes were red, and her cheeks were wet.

"I wasn't uncomfortable."

Her eyes widened, confusion shifting to what looked like longing. His stomach dipped and swirled as attraction zipped along his nerve endings like wildfire. His gaze dipped to her lips, and he suddenly wanted to test their softness.

She put a staying hand on his chest. "I find that hard to believe, Mr. Evasive."

Releasing her, he passed his hand over his face. The tips of his ears burned. What had he been thinking? He couldn't kiss this woman.

"Mr. Evasive, huh?"

"You're one of the most closemouthed people I've ever met. Did you ever tell Lucy about your father's mistreatment?"

His head reared back, defensive walls flying up. "How do you know about that?"

"It's nothing to be ashamed of. Did you reconcile before his death?"

He gritted his teeth and quickly stood.

"I guess not," she said, her voice full of speculation.

"Is that why you're so determined to expand the ranch? To prove him wrong?"

Nash winced. How had she cut to the heart of the matter so easily?

"We should go."

"You're right. We should."

The closeness between them evaporated like smoke.

This was a good reminder of their stark differences. Granted, he'd invited her confidence moments earlier, but he hadn't blasted her with questions about things he knew nothing about. The accident and aftermath were common knowledge. His relationship with his father was not.

Skye had poked and prodded him like an ornery bull, trying to force him to reveal his most private thoughts and feelings. He was more comfortable ignoring them. Going forward, he'd also be ignoring her effect on him.

TWELVE

An apology hovered on Skye's lips, but the words refused to come. The miles back to Tulip rolled by in silence, the spring-green rural scenery wasted on them. Eden was on the verge of sleep, and Nash was staring out the passenger window. He alternately massaged his thigh and temples, a constant grimace on his tense face. Guilt nipped at her. He'd accompanied her to the facility despite his injury, and she'd repaid his kindness with a verbal assault.

The truth was that the feelings Nash aroused in her were frightening. She'd had to do *something* to shock them out of the force drawing them together. He'd seen her at her most vulnerable and hadn't run. He'd invited her confidence and listened without judgment. He'd made her feel like he was on her side, like she wasn't in this fight alone. His strong arms had sheltered her while she'd cried out her frustration, and his steady heartbeat beneath her cheek had been reassuring. She could've stayed there for the rest of the day. When he'd stared deeply into her eyes, his face inches from hers and fingers hot against her skin, she'd almost let herself forget how very wrong anything romantic between them would be.

Nash Wilder had always belonged to Lucy. Now he was forever linked to her through the child they'd created. Besides, Skye couldn't let herself depend on anyone but herself. She liked being in control. Leaning on someone else was risky. It led to a vicious, repetitive cycle of hopes raised and dashed. After her mother's death, Skye had resolved to avoid that.

She slowed as they entered the downtown district. There were plenty of shoppers out on this beautiful Sunday, along with congregants of the church spilling from the historic building. Nash would've attended services if not for her visit with Dove. Skye would've had to go along to provide protection. She had mixed feelings about her struggles with God, but now, more than ever, she craved peace.

"Pull over." Nash pointed to the Pit Stop Café. "That's Bubba's truck."

Skye parked the truck in an empty spot near the bookstore.

Eden lifted her head and looked around. "Waffle?"

Nash glanced at his watch. "It is lunchtime. We can grab something to eat and speak to Bubba."

Inside the café, the waitress behind the counter told them to seat themselves. The breakfast rush had ended, and the lunch crowd hadn't yet arrived. Most of the bar stools and tables were vacant, and the empty booths had yet to be cleared of dishes and wiped clean. Holding Eden, Nash nodded to the far corner booth where Bubba sat with his back to the door.

Skye led the way. "Bubba. Just the man I wanted to see."

She slid into the seat without waiting for an invitation.

Bubba narrowed his eyes. He glared first at her, then at Nash, who remained standing.

He lowered a slice of bacon onto his plate and wiped his fingers with his napkin. "What do you want?"

Skye leaned forward and locked her hands together on the table. "Information."

"I told you—"

"Were you and Lucy a couple?"

His eyes widened slightly. "Where'd you get that idea?"

"Answer the question."

"No." He stared at her without blinking. "We were not a couple."

Skye studied him, trying to decide if she believed him. There was something in his eyes, something she couldn't pin down.

"You're grasping at straws, Deputy. Don't try to pin Tulip's troubles on me. You can't take care of yourself. What makes you think you can take care of this town?"

The barb stung. Was that what people thought of her? It wasn't easy to keep her expression blank.

Nash moved closer. "That was uncalled for."

"If I find out you're lying, Bubba, I'll charge you with obstruction," she said.

He glowered at her, picked up his fork and shoveled scrambled eggs into his mouth, a sign he was done talking.

Nash touched her elbow as she shuffled out of the booth. "What do you say we take our food to go?"

Skye agreed. Their order didn't take long to prepare, and they were soon on their way back to the ranch.

"What's your take on Bubba?" Nash asked.

She kept her gaze on the road. "He's hiding something."

"You think they were involved?"

"Do you?" she countered.

"Undecided. I agree he's keeping something from us. Whether or not it would be useful to the case is another story."

"I'll have to take a closer look at his personal life." She sighed. "I'll try to be discreet, but I can't guarantee he won't find out or that it won't anger him and his father."

"Do what you have to do."

Back at the ranch, they found Maeve's Cadillac in the drive, the woman herself ensconced in a porch chair.

"Were you expecting her?" Skye asked, turning off the engine.

Nash's brows dipped. "No, ma'am."

As they exited the vehicle, Maeve rose gracefully to her feet. She wore a peach dress and a matching wide-brimmed hat that shaded the top half of her face.

"I heard you were shot," she said without preamble, her wide gaze locked on Nash. "Why did I have to hear it from my garden club members?"

A sigh rumbled through his chest as he unbuckled Eden. "I've been a bit preoccupied, Maeve."

Skye glanced between them and decided to excuse herself. "I have an errand to run."

"Remember the bulls are arriving tonight for tomorrow's rodeo," Nash said. "I have to be there."

"I'll be back in time."

Before anyone could ask questions, she started walking back to where her cruiser was parked. She couldn't handle any more family drama today.

The bull-riding event Nash was sponsoring was held in neighboring Farmdale. Although she'd accompanied him here last night as he'd overseen the bulls' arrival and checked to make sure the permits had been secured, she hadn't fully grasped the scope of the event. Pulling into the gravel parking area ringing the stands the following evening, she frowned at the sea of cars, trucks and trailers. Cowboys on horseback wound through the thick crowd streaming in to find seats or to purchase snacks from the food vendors in the adjacent field. This was a security nightmare, and she told him so.

He rounded the front of the truck and braced one hand on the hood. Decked out in a black Stetson, crisp black-and-white Western shirt, clean jeans and boots, his belt buckle the size of a salad plate, he was the epitome of cowboy cool. His skin bore the stamp of the Mississippi sun, and he had various small scars, nicks and scrapes earned from working the land. His body was lean, his muscles rock-hard from his never-ending list of chores.

Her mouth went dry, even though she'd been in his company nonstop for days. Holding her yesterday, he'd stroked her hair. She wanted the same freedom, to test the blond strands between her fingertips. His freshly shaved cheeks begged to be framed between her palms. And his mouth… Would it be soft against hers? Or firm and demanding?

His eyes crinkled at the corners as he surveyed the bustling scene. "If I could've bowed out, I would've. But this is only my second year hosting, and I have to prove to our current sponsors that I can make this a success. Plus, we have a potential sponsor here tonight. She owns a property management company, and she's considering becoming our largest supporter in next year's event."

"This is too much, especially since Hank and Chen are on the opposite end of the county at that warehouse fire."

She'd counted on having them here as backup. The attack on Nash was fresh in her mind, and her pulse skittered in dread. What if Lucy's killer had followed them here? He could easily blend in with this crowd.

"It's not ideal, I know," he said, his mouth tight. "We'll stay in the organizers' booth the entire time. I'll have an unobstructed view of the stands and pens. We'll be able to see any potential threats."

Skye clamped her mouth shut. It was her job to protect him, and he didn't always make it easy. At least Eden was safe at the ranch. Maeve's ruffled feathers had been smoothed, according to Nash, by the offer of uninterrupted time with her granddaughter.

As they climbed the stands toward the booth, several people waylaid Nash, wanting a word or handshake. Almost at the top, Skye spotted a familiar face.

Nash went into the booth, but Skye hung back.

"Hello, Grace."

The petite blonde had been speaking to the woman beside her, and she lifted her head at Skye's greeting. Was her smile a bit tight?

"Hello, Deputy."

"Is this your first time at the rodeo?"

She nodded. "Nash mentioned he was one of the organizers. I live right down the road from here." She swiveled her head. "Where's Eden?"

"With her grandmother."

"Oh." After a beat, she motioned to the space beside her. "You're welcome to sit with us, if you want."

"Thank you, but I'll be in the booth with Nash."

The woman's eyes got a guarded look. "Well, I'll see you around."

Skye went to join Nash, trying to figure out the reason she had taken an almost instant dislike of Grace Thompson. Surely, it wasn't because the girl had an obvious crush on Nash? Disgusted with herself, she entered the booth and offered a perfunctory smile as Nash introduced her to the announcer and the other two organizers.

The hired country music group continued to play as a horse and rider trotted around the central arena bearing the US flag. Rodeo clowns gathered in one corner while riders in the lineup for bulls perched on the pens. Giant lights were bright against the darkened sky.

"The sponsors will be pleased with this turnout," Nash said, coming to stand beside her. There was a hint of relief in his voice.

One hand on the railing, she tilted her head to study his profile. "Why is this event important to you? You've got your hands full with the ranch and cattle company."

"I got involved because it not only supports bull riders, but because I need to generate revenue that isn't dependent on my physical abilities. Ranching is hard on the body, and you never know when an injury could sideline you. Maybe for good. Now that I have a daughter to support, this sort of thing will be more important than ever."

She admired his devotion to the family name and heritage, and that he was committed to giving Eden a solid future.

"You ever think about bull riding?"

His teeth flashed under the bright lights. "Maybe for a minute. My father squashed that idea real quick."

The announcer came to ask Nash some questions, and they drifted over to the long table set up to hold paperwork and assorted folders. Skye went back to surveying the crowd, looking for anyone who stood out. Soon, the music stopped, and the announcer's voice boomed into the night, welcoming the attendees to the clamor of hoots, hollers and claps.

The noise swelled as the first rider dropped into place on the bull's back, gave the signal and barreled through the open gate. He managed to stay on for three seconds before being tossed to the earth. Obviously not a novice, he rolled out of the way and hustled to the sidelines.

Skye's stomach rumbled. She waited until she couldn't

ignore the hunger pangs and then went to Nash. "I'm going to get a hot dog. You want anything?"

"I'll take one, too." He reached for his wallet, and she put her hand out to stop him.

"It's my treat."

He would've argued but was distracted by the announcer.

Skye left the booth, descended the stairs and strode to the hot dog stand, her gaze roaming over the people as she went. The line was ridiculous, however, and she wasn't comfortable being gone for too long. She walked along the row, finally veering to the last hot dog vendor. The truck was parked at a different angle than the rest, so she had to go around the side to find the window. There were three people ahead of her, but the girl taking the orders and payment was efficient.

Skye placed her order and moved off to the side to wait, noting the parked gray passenger van, beat-up truck and church bus at her back. As the other waiting customers received their orders, Skye pulled out her phone to check for messages and registered movement directly behind her.

Before she could turn, something hard connected with her skull. She tumbled against the van. A second blow struck above her ear, and she sank into darkness.

THIRTEEN

Why wasn't Skye answering? Fifteen minutes had stretched into twenty, and Nash had started to get antsy. When he got her voice mail again, he exited the booth and started to descend the stairs.

"Nash?" Grace snagged his sleeve. "Is something wrong?"

"I can't reach Skye. I think she might be in trouble."

She pressed her hand to her chest. "Is there anything I can do?"

"I'm going to check the vendors. Would you mind going to the portable bathrooms?"

"Sure."

"Text me if you find her."

Nash hurried to the bottom of the stands and out into the adjacent field. He didn't see her at the hot dog vendor, nor at the neighboring pretzel trailer. His heart climbed into his throat as he continued past the others and still couldn't find her. Tall, lithe and striking, she wasn't one to blend in with the crowd. What color had she been wearing? His mind went blank.

Calm yourself, Wilder. She's a cop. She can handle herself.

But why would she ignore my calls?

At the end of the row, he stopped, pivoted and surveyed the fields. The next bull rider launched into the
arena as the crowd gasped and cheered. Nash had been
preoccupied tonight with his burning need to make this
a success and impress the potential sponsor. He'd let his
focus slip from what was truly important.

Pulling up the sheriff's department's website on his
phone, he scrolled through until he landed on her photo
and then returned to the first hot dog vendor.

Walking to the side of the food truck, he stepped into
the open doorway, startling the cook and his helper.

"Have you seen this woman?" He thrust his phone
toward them.

They both shook their heads, their expressions baffled.

"I'm Nash Wilder, one of the organizers. This woman
is a deputy and a friend of mine. I think she may be in
a bind. Can you take a second look? Are you sure she
didn't order from you?"

The female bent closer, squinting at the photo. "I don't
recognize her. We've had a crush of customers, though."

He thanked them and moved next door. His anxiety
built with each negative answer he received. At the last
one, he repeated his questions.

The cook shrugged. "I've got my nose to the grill,
man. No time to interact with customers."

The young woman taking orders clipped a ticket to the
grill hood and came closer for a look. Her brow puckered.
"I saw her. She was here not long ago. Ordered hot dogs
and sodas, but she never picked them up." She nodded
to the items sitting on the counter. "I placed them there
in case she came back."

A fresh sense of urgency gripped him. "You didn't see
which way she went, did you?"

"No. I'm sorry."

Nash dashed between the vehicles parked close to the vendor, praying Skye had perhaps been roped into providing assistance to someone. Medical emergencies happened all the time. But the ambulance on standby was dark, and there was no activity around it. He returned to the vendor and again searched the space around it, paying closer attention to the ground this time. He activated his phone light. Would she show up and laugh his concern away? Maybe she'd bumped into an old friend and had gotten caught up in conversation. If that was the case, she was going to have some serious making up to do.

The beam glinted on something shiny close to the van's tire. Skye's duty badge. Thunder pulsed in his ears. He tried to contain his panic, but then a text came through from Grace. Skye wasn't at the bathrooms.

He dialed 9-1-1 on his way to his truck. If the killer had managed to grab her unnoticed, he'd want to get her as far away as possible—and quickly. Spraying gravel as he left the lot, he drove in the opposite direction of Tulip, toward the interstate ramp.

He relayed his suspicions to the dispatcher, who promised to send authorities to the event site. Nash disconnected and called Skye's phone again.

This time, it didn't go to voice mail.

"Nash, I need help."

His stomach plunged to his feet, and his heart flipped over. She didn't sound good. Her voice was hushed. Scratchy.

"Where are you?"

"In a moving vehicle. A car."

"Is he there with you?"

"He's driving. I'm in the trunk."

Fury fused with the fear sliding through his veins. He deliberately blocked the thoughts racing down dark avenues. "Listen to me, Skye. I'm in my truck searching for you. I've already contacted the authorities. Are your hands and legs free?"

"Yes." He heard shuffling and her breath hiss over the speaker.

"What is it?" he demanded, his truck barreling along the deserted stretch of pavement.

"I'm okay. He struck my head when he took me, and it hurts." More movement. "I'm going to try to push out a taillight."

"Can you find an emergency trunk release lever?"

There was a long silence. "I don't think there is one."

"It's probably an older-model car." If the car was outfitted with a cable trunk release near the driver's seat, Skye could possibly pull the cable and open the trunk latch. "Here's what I want you to do. Pull up the carpet and feel for a cable. Start on the driver's side."

She grunted, and he could picture her in a dark, tight space, injured and at the mercy of a killer. Nash ground his teeth together and applied more pressure to the gas pedal. This had to work.

"I can't find it. It's not here, Nash." Although her voice was strained, she was still in control.

"That's okay. You'll find it. Search the sides."

The minutes stretched like years. He scoured the side roads as he passed. When the interstate ramp loomed ahead, he faced a decision.

"Skye, are you going fast enough to be on the interstate?"

"I'm not sure."

Nash applied the brakes, ready to take the turn.

"I found it!" Before he could give her instructions, she gasped. "We're slowing down. Do you think he heard me? My weapon's missing, Nash. He probably took it for himself or tossed it."

His fingers clenched the phone.

There was a bumping sound. "Skye, talk to me."

"We're speeding up again." Relief coated her words. "We bounced over something hard and uneven. It could be railroad tracks. The train runs through Farmdale near the depot."

He pressed his foot on the gas again, regaining speed. "I'm three miles from there. Listen, Skye, pull the cable toward the front of the car. That should open the trunk."

She gasped again. "It worked. I'm going to jump."

"Wait—"

The sounds after that were muffled, and then the line went dead.

Skye rolled into the grass, lungs heaving and adrenaline churning. She stared up at the moonless sky and sucked in great gulps of fresh air. The inside of her abductor's trunk had smelled like rotten meat and cat litter.

At the downshifting of an engine, dread zipped through her sore, aching body, and she shifted onto her stomach, desperate to stay hidden. The taillight she hadn't busted out gleamed a menacing red. For a split second, she thought he was going to stop in the middle of the road. If he did, could she manage to outrun him?

Would he notice the open trunk, given that it was dark?

Skye turned to look in the direction they'd just come from. Where was Nash? When she turned to scan the car again, her heart nearly leaped out of her chest. It had coasted to the shoulder. The driver had stopped the car. Opened the door.

Skye started scrambling backward. She wasn't going back into that trunk. Wasn't going to submit to his evil whims.

Powerful twin beams sliced through the night, punctuated by the rumble of a heavy-duty truck coming up the road fast. The car door slammed shut. The driver peeled onto the road and made a sharp right onto a side street farther down.

Pushing off the ground, Skye waved her arms over her head and jogged toward the truck. It veered to the shoulder, and Nash emerged seconds later. She'd never been so happy to see anyone in her life. He urged her into the truck through his open driver's-side door. When she started to scoot over, he clamped his hand on her knee, keeping her right beside him in the middle of the row seat.

"He went that way." She pointed. "Let's catch up with him."

"What happened?" Nash ground out, putting the truck into gear. "I looked everywhere for you. If I hadn't found your badge…"

His profile was illuminated by the dash lights. He was worried about her. Because he considered her another of his responsibilities? Or because he also felt the growing closeness between them?

"After I placed my order, I stood off to the side to wait. The couple ahead of me got their food and left. The workers inside the truck wouldn't have been able to see me from that angle, so our man took a chance. There was a bus that would've blocked anyone else from seeing us." She rubbed at her sore head, glad there was only a small knot and no broken skin.

He took the same turn as her abductor and sped past cornfields. She contacted Dispatch and requested help in the search. She hadn't gotten a license plate number and couldn't be certain of the make or model. All she had was the busted taillight. Time was of the essence.

Farmland eventually gave way to neighborhoods and the occasional gas station. The more populated area would provide her abductor with multiple places to hide. Skye's hopes began to flag.

"What's that?"

Leaning forward over the wheel, he applied the brakes and nodded to the flash of red and blue lights on their right. Turning into a short alley between brick buildings, they parked behind a sheriff's car and fire truck. Firefighters were scrambling to respond to the emergency— a car engulfed in flames.

The deputy from this neighboring county recognized Skye and acknowledged her with a nod and brief greeting.

"What happened?" she asked.

He shrugged. "Witness called in a fire. Not sure of the cause yet. Doesn't look like it's been wrecked."

Nash's grim gaze met hers. "Are you thinking what I'm thinking?"

She fisted her hands. "He got away again, and he made sure to leave very little evidence behind."

FOURTEEN

Sleep was elusive that night. Nash rehashed everything from the moment they arrived at the rodeo to the discovery of the torched car. Although Skye was safe, he couldn't relax. When he heard her rummaging in the kitchen, he pulled a shirt on over his head and went to check on her.

"Can't sleep?" he greeted her in a hushed voice.

She jerked, spilling milk on the counter.

"Sorry." He mopped it up with a paper towel.

"I didn't hear you come in. I was lost in my own head."

The hood light above the stove allowed him to see her tense features. Wearing a midthigh-length pink shirt over black leggings, her face free of makeup and her ebony hair a cascade of curls, she looked nothing like the self-assured cop he was used to. She looked vulnerable and scared.

Nash placed his hands on her shoulders and gently turned her toward the couch. "Have a seat. I'll make us a snack."

She tucked into one corner of the couch and pulled a thin blanket around her, holding the corners together at her neck. He poured them both milk and rummaged in the cabinets until he found chocolate sandwich cookies not yet past their expiration date. After arranging everything on the coffee table and turning on the side lamp, he pulled a dining chair over and sat facing her.

She dunked a cookie into the milk before taking a bite. When she didn't initiate conversation, he rested his elbows on his knees. "What's our next step?"

"Talk to locals and see if anyone can corroborate Virgil's claims about Bubba and Lucy. The car was probably stolen. They're supposed to let us know if they recover the VIN number."

After leaving the scene, they'd returned to the rodeo and spoken to that county's sheriff and deputies. "Maybe a witness will come forward."

"Maybe."

Unable to resist her defeated expression, he crossed to the couch and angled his body toward her.

"I'm sorry that he's turned his sights on you."

"I'm the equivalent of a hired bodyguard. Makes sense he'd want me out of the way. One less barrier to his target." She turned her head and looked straight at him. "He didn't win tonight, and that's thanks to you."

He folded his hand around hers and brought it to rest on his thigh. "God was with us."

Her expression turned wistful. "I wish I had that kind of faith. I've felt abandoned by Him most of my life. Honoria talks about His care and provision, about how He gives her the strength to get through hard times. I can't relate."

He searched for the right words to say. "My mom used to talk about Jesus like He was her best friend. I never could understand it. As I got older, and the emptiness inside me couldn't be filled with relationships, hobbies or work, I remembered things my mom had said. I spoke with a Christian buddy of mine in my platoon, and he pointed me to scripture passages that answered my questions. After a few weeks, I was ready to put my faith in Christ. I've never regretted my decision to follow Him. Life isn't easy, but He has promised to strengthen and guide us, to comfort us."

Skye clung to his hand.

He rubbed his thumb across her knuckles in a gentle back-and-forth caress. Nash would fix things for her if he could. Her weakened faith. Her living situation. Her sister's medical needs. He wished his problems hadn't compounded hers, but he couldn't regret the changes between them. She no longer saw him as a heartless ogre— or, at least, he didn't think she did. He'd been gifted with a glimpse into what made Skye Saddler tick, and he could view the past with a clearer understanding now.

"Would you like to pray together?" he ventured.

She bit her lip. "I don't think I can. Will you?"

Feeling inadequate, he prayed for God's protection and a quick resolution to the case. When he finished, he noticed a tear snaking down her cheek. He reached up and wiped the teardrop with his thumb. "What are you thinking?"

Her big green eyes drank him in. "You wouldn't believe me if I told you."

His heart did a triple backflip. He inched closer, wary and fascinated at the same time. Her thoughts were a mystery, and Nash desperately wanted to unravel them.

"Try me."

She gripped his wrist and slowly lowered his hand. "Not tonight, cowboy."

"You've been free with your opinions. Why clam up now? Scared?"

"Embarrassed." Her gaze swept to her lap, and she plucked at the blanket seams. "You mentioned your marine buddy, and that got me to thinking about your time in boot camp. The thing is, I sent you a nasty letter while you were there. I regretted it as soon as I mailed it. I've always hoped it got lost somewhere between Tulip and Parris Island."

He sank against the cushions like a deflated balloon. "It didn't get lost. I was surprised to get it because not many people besides Remi sent me letters."

Her three-page missive had outlined his failings in detail. Not exactly what he'd needed to hear while trying to survive boot camp. But beneath her anger had been hurt and deep concern for her friend. Lucy's poor choices had begun to pile up, and Skye had been rightfully worried. He'd been worried, too, but there wasn't a thing he could've done about it at that point.

Grimacing, she lifted her gaze once more. "I'm sorry, Nash. I shouldn't have written those things. It wasn't my place."

"You're a fine champion of causes, Deputy Saddler. It's a good trait to have. I'm glad you're still fighting for Lucy."

Her fingers skimmed his leg. "For you, too. And for Eden."

Her message was loud and clear—this was no longer a case she was assigned. This was personal. He was grateful for her loyalty and devotion, even though he didn't know whether or not he deserved it.

Her phone pinged, and she skimmed through the text. "Deputy Fernandez, the one at the fire, said they found a jug of gasoline near the scene. They're going to try to get prints."

Nash's gut hardened. Her abductor had obviously come prepared to do away with her and destroy the evidence. She was his protector. Now he was unofficially hers.

* * *

"You're not coming in my house." Bubba Chesterfield blocked the door to the home he shared with his father, his arms crossed over his barrel chest and booted feet planted wide.

His father, stationed at the bottom of the steps, stared up at him. "They have a warrant, son. We have no choice."

Skye rested one hand on her waist, near her service weapon. While she didn't expect a violent confrontation, she'd learned in recent days to be ready for anything. Chen and Flowers were here to help search. They had initially been skeptical about a link between Bubba and Lucy. However, she'd told them about the tip she and Nash had gotten that morning from Kayla, a waitress at the Pit Stop who'd claimed to have seen Bubba and Lucy at the bowling alley together.

Skye and Nash had gone over and spoken with the owner, who'd confirmed the tip. According to him, Bubba and Lucy had been in a handful of times within the last year. They didn't bowl. They bought snacks and hung out in the arcade room, which was conveniently out of sight. The owner insisted Eden hadn't been with them.

Bubba's nostrils flared as he leveled his gaze at Skye. She lifted her chin and returned his stare steadily, hoping her fluttering heartbeat and the sweat on her brow weren't noticeable. Based on his size and strength, Bubba could've easily and quickly subdued her and stowed her in that trunk. Was he the one who'd stabbed Lucy, shot Nash and abducted her?

"You can tell Wilder the land deal is off." He stomped down the stairs and shoved past her, almost knocking her over.

Zane frowned at her. "You have my permission to

pass on my son's message. We're no longer interested in doing business."

Skye felt terrible. Nash had been eager for this deal, and now he'd lost his chance at expansion.

Chen charged past the older man. Skye and Hank followed him into the house and divvied up the rooms. Chen chose Bubba's. Searching through another person's home would never feel comfortable. Remembering Lucy's last moments helped her refocus. Her friend deserved justice, no matter the identity of the perpetrator.

When she came up empty, she entered Bubba's room. "Find anything?"

Chen had pulled out the drawers of the desk and was searching through assorted papers. "Not a thing." His stare was full of reproach.

"Have you gone through the closet yet?"

"Go ahead."

Inside the small, surprisingly tidy closet, there were clothes and old boot- and hatboxes. Chen tossed the last handful of papers on the desk in disgust. "Looks like a waste of our time, not to mention the Chesterfields'."

Skye pressed her lips together to keep from spouting off the various retorts springing to mind.

"Clean this up," he told her, pivoting toward the door.

Hank blocked his exit, his expression triumphant. "Look what I found."

Chen snatched the photograph from Hank's grasp and brought it close to his face.

"What is it?" Skye asked, moving closer.

Posture rigid, the sergeant held it out without looking at her. "We need to have a chat with Bubba down at the station."

She took the photo that was dated within the last year.

"They look cozy, don't they?" Hank commented.

"Sure do," she agreed.

Bubba and Lucy were grinning at the camera, his arm slung around her waist. The wooded background didn't give clues as to their location.

"Where did you find this?"

"Tucked in one of the bathroom drawers, beneath a pile of deodorant sticks and a can of shaving cream."

Skye and Hank exited the house behind Chen. Zane and Bubba, who'd found shade near the old Chevelle, stopped their conversation to stare at them.

"Not a good idea to lie to the police," Chen snapped. "You're coming to the station for an official interview, Bubba."

Zane's expression revealed surprise. "What's he talking about, son?"

Bubba's face flushed. "I haven't done anything wrong."

Chen directed Bubba into the back of his cruiser. After texting Nash the update, Skye followed Chen to the station.

Their setup was too small to have an interrogation room. Chen perched on the edge of his desk and pointed Bubba into the chair facing it. Skye stood to the side with a good view of both men.

"Where were you last night between the hours of seven and ten p.m.?"

"At home."

"Can anyone vouch for you?"

"I was watching television. Alone. Dad was at a friend's house."

"What about the night Nash Wilder got shot?"

"Don't remember."

"Tell us about you and Lucy Ackerman."

Bubba shifted in his chair. "We were friends, all right?"

"You hid that information from us because…"

"I didn't want you thinking I killed her." His eyes heated, and he balled his fists. "I would *never* hurt her."

"Tell us about your relationship. From all accounts, you weren't in the same social circles. How did you become close? How often did you see her?"

He swallowed hard. "We ran into each other down in Biloxi a while back and had dinner. Lucy was easy to talk to. I reminded her of home. We agreed to meet up again, and it became a regular thing. We saw each other a couple of times a month, mostly in Biloxi or somewhere in between. She only came here when ranch business prevented me from leaving Tulip."

"Why sneak around?"

"Lucy wanted to avoid her mom."

Skye snorted. "More like she wanted to avoid Nash. I assume she told you about Eden?"

Bubba's upper lip curled. "Sure, I knew. What of it?"

"Nash deserved to know he had a daughter," she retorted, unable to keep the disgust from her voice.

"Wasn't my place to tell him."

Skye was convinced that was the main reason for Bubba's hostility toward Nash. The land deal had irked him, but Nash's link to Lucy was the true sticking point.

"Did romance enter the picture?" Chen asked.

His mouth drooped, and he shook his head.

"You wanted more," Skye interjected, earning a sideways glance from Chen. "But she didn't."

"I didn't kill her," he reiterated, spreading his hands wide.

"Is Saddler right?" Chen said. "Did you want a romantic relationship with Lucy?"

He jutted his chin. "I loved her."

"I see." Chen tilted his head and crossed his arms.

"How did you feel when she rejected you? Angry enough to want revenge?"

Skye watched the emotions play over Bubba's face. Spurned love was one motive for murder. Could he have gotten so upset that things got out of hand? Lucy's violent death suggested strong emotion on the part of her killer.

"Here's what I think…" Chen began. "You and Lucy met at that abandoned house. You told her how you felt, and she laughed you off. You couldn't take it, so you ended her, right then and there."

Bubba shot out of the chair so fast that Chen reared back, nearly falling off the desk.

"I did no such thing!" he roared.

Skye withdrew her weapon and ordered him to stand down. Bubba opened and closed his fists, his jaw working and steam practically shooting from his ears. Chen stood up and glowered at the taller, stockier man.

"Unless you want things to get ugly, I'd do as she says."

Bubba kicked the desk before resuming his seat. After several tense minutes, Skye returned her weapon to its holster.

"She was dating someone," he admitted with a defeated air. "Before you ask, I don't know who. She wouldn't say."

Chen's face reflected surprise. "Did she give you any hints?"

"Only that he was older. She claimed to love him but suspected he was playing mind games. I told her to drop him, that she deserved better, but she wouldn't listen. He's the one you should be looking into, not me."

Skye leaned against the wall. Could this be true? Lucy's roommate thought she'd had a boyfriend. If it wasn't Bubba, then who?

FIFTEEN

Back at the ranch, Skye parked her cruiser near the two-lane highway and began the short walk to the house. The cows must be grazing in a distant pasture because the area closest to the road was unoccupied except for a pair of brown rabbits. A pair of ducks skimmed across the pond's surface. The Wilder Ranch was a beautiful slice of southern Mississippi. Although she didn't particularly like the occasional whiff of cow dung baking in the sun, she was going to miss the ranch once this case was solved. Wherever she landed, it wouldn't compare to this place. And it wouldn't have Nash.

As she got closer to the calf barn, she heard voices and laughter. She ducked between the fence slats and strode through the grass. Through the open door, she could see Grace giving Eden a piggyback ride. She jogged in circles, gently bouncing the toddler and evoking delighted laughter. Nash was relaxed against a stall, arms and ankles crossed, his blue eyes bright and an indulgent smile on his face.

Skye's heart dropped like a stone. With their matching fair hair and complexions, they looked like they belonged together. A natural family. Was Nash aware that Grace liked him? Did he return her feelings?

Hovering nearby, she wrestled with overwhelming sadness and a sense of loss that didn't make sense. Nash Wilder had never been hers. She hadn't wanted him to be. Now she wasn't sure what she wanted. Surely, not to have a permanent place in Nash's and Eden's lives. Skye didn't deserve that kind of happiness. She'd had a family once and she'd failed them one too many times. That failure had destroyed everything.

She released the breath she'd been holding and saw Nash straighten as his gaze located her. His forehead creased. "Skye?"

Grace stopped her play and blew a curl out of her eyes. Her smile faded.

Carefully controlling her expression, Skye stepped into the space. "Sorry to interrupt. I was on my way to the house and heard voices…" She shrugged, feeling her face heat. Where was her usual poise?

Eden squirmed, and Grace lowered the girl to the ground. The toddler ran over, threw her arms around Skye's legs and grinned up at her. "Waffles?"

Her heart melted. She cupped Eden's face. "I don't know what the supper plans are just yet."

"I brought chili," Grace interrupted, tucking her hair behind her ears. "I made a large batch last night."

Nash shoved off the stall and came closer. "Grace, I need to speak with Skye. Would you mind taking Eden into the house?"

The gaze she shot him could only be described as adoring. "Of course."

Once they had left, Nash shoved his hands in his jeans' pockets and studied her somberly. "Is Bubba our man?"

"Hard to say. His whereabouts for the last two attacks can't be confirmed, but he swears he's innocent."

"Do you believe him?"

"I believe he cared about Lucy. Whether or not he let his emotions get the better of him remains to be seen."

Nash lifted his hat and ran his fingers through his hair. "You don't have enough to hold him, though."

"The guns we found in the Chesterfield residence didn't match the one used on you. We can't link that burned-out car to him, either."

"If only we'd had security cameras at the rodeo last night."

"We still haven't ruled out Virgil. I need to talk to Maeve again." She regretted that this investigation was making his personal life difficult. "Zane and Bubba gave me a message to pass along. The deal is off."

"I figured."

"I'm sorry. I know how much it meant to you."

"How do you feel about a ride?"

"On a horse?"

He grinned. "Would you prefer my tractor?"

"It's been a while since I was in the saddle."

"I'll give you a docile mount."

"Grace won't mind?"

"She said she didn't have plans tonight."

"That was a hint."

"Huh?"

"She wants to spend the evening with you, Nash."

Skye watched as understanding dawned. Try as she might, she couldn't pin down how he felt about it. "It's obvious she has feelings for you. Would you be open to a relationship with her?"

His eyebrows crashed together, and his gaze became very intense. Stepping into her personal space, he brought his hands up to frame her face. Skye's heart thumped, and her knees went weak.

He lowered his lips to hers in a kiss that deepened almost instantly. This was no slow introduction. This was a cowboy who knew what he wanted, and he was branding her as his. It was over almost as soon as it began. He looked as shocked as she felt.

She pressed her fingers to her mouth, trying to hold on to the moment for as long as possible. Why had he kissed her? What did it mean? Did he regret it? Did she?

This man used to belong to her best friend. What would Lucy think?

"I've been mulling over an idea, and I'd like to run it by you," he said carefully, showing his palms. "Just promise you won't freak out."

Skye's senses were reeling from the kiss and she could only nod.

"As you already know, my relationship with my father became strained after my mom died. Life with him was…" His forehead creased. "Well, let's just say I dreaded being around him. I couldn't do anything right. He criticized everything—my appearance, my grades, my choice of friends, my work on the ranch. There was no pleasing him. He's the reason I joined the Marines right out of high school, the reason I turned my back on my heritage for so long."

Skye wasn't sure where this was going. Although she was thrilled he was opening up to her, she could tell his words were dragged from a private, painful place. "Lucy never could figure out why you lit out of Tulip. She thought it was to get away from her."

"During our last conversation, I thought about telling her how bad things had gotten. I wasn't sure how she'd react. It had seemed pointless since I was leaving Tulip regardless."

"It must've been tough to endure all that, especially after losing your mom."

"My mom was amazing. She was my biggest cheer-leader and sounding board. I wish I'd had her for longer."

Skye remembered being at Glory Wilder's funeral. Thirteen-year-old Nash had stuck close to his younger sister, comforting her throughout the somber service. Skye had thought Wes a cold, austere man. He hadn't shed a single tear, and he'd seemed almost embarrassed by his children's grief.

"Were you able to reconcile before his death?"

His face shadowed. "How do you reconcile with some-one who considers you a complete and utter failure? I didn't measure up to Wilder standards. He was glad to be rid of me."

"Is that why you're driven to put your own stamp on the ranch? To build it bigger and better?"

"Yes." He didn't try to deny it. "I know it's irrational, but I have to prove to myself that he was wrong."

She rubbed his arm. "You're no failure, Nash Wilder. You're an astute businessman, a hardworking cowboy and a wonderful father."

His eyes were as clear as the ocean. "Your opinion of me has undergone a radical change."

She licked her dry lips and wondered if he might kiss her again.

"I didn't figure a family was in my future, but now I have a daughter to raise. I'll do anything to protect Eden and give her a loving, nurturing home." He took her hand. "Eden needs a mother. Someone who'll fight for her. Someone like you."

Her jaw sagged. "What are you saying?"

"I think we should get married. It will solve all of our problems. Eden will have a mother. You'll have a home. I'll provide for Dove. You'll never have to worry about her having the proper care."

Skye stared at him, unable to speak for long moments.

He squeezed her hand. "It's unconventional, but I'm certain we can make a good life together."

"You want a babysitter," she spluttered, "not a wife."

"That's not true. I'd be proud to have you as my wife."

His words washed her addled brain in delight. "What about love?"

His brow creased. "Isn't friendship enough? I'm no good at romance, Skye. I can provide a safe, stable home life. A happy home for Eden."

Skye searched his face, her heart hurting. He saw her as a solution to a problem.

"Not that long ago, you and I weren't even on speaking terms."

"We weren't enemies, though, Skye. Truth is, we really didn't know each other. We only thought we did."

"I can't marry you."

"Do you have reservations about ranch life? I wouldn't expect you to give up your career."

"This proposal, this whole idea, was born out of desperation. Nash, you will find a way to raise Eden on your own. You don't need me or anyone else." The thought that he might pose this same question to Grace made her stomach churn. "I refuse to become the biggest regret of your life, and you would regret it eventually."

Honoria dumped onions and garlic into the giant pot of boiling water. Skye cut the lemons one by one and squeezed in the juice before tossing them in, her thoughts tumbling over each other like the crawfish boil ingredients. She'd left Nash alone in the barn, called Hank to guard him and fled to her closest friend's home. She usually didn't have trouble sharing her thoughts with anyone, especially Honoria. But the words were jammed up inside with all the confusing emotions.

She shook in a copious amount of cayenne pepper and replaced the lid.

The breeze shifting through her friend's expansive yard softened the sun's bite. Honoria held out a soda as they moved deeper into the shade. The patio door slapped open, and her husband, Leo, began draping old newspapers over the wooden picnic table. Their shaggy beast of a dog zipped out behind him and made a beeline for Skye.

Crouching, she accepted Jupiter's friendly kisses while holding her drink out of reach.

"I think he likes you better than me," Honoria quipped. "He's never forgotten how you rescued him."

Thanks to the errant pup, a friendship had been born that night long ago.

Skye had been heading home after a shift and had noticed a car stalled on the road's shoulder. Oblivious to the pelting rain, Honoria had flagged Skye down. The storm had spooked Jupiter, and he'd slipped out of the car at the nearby gas station. Honoria had spotted him in the vicinity, but he wasn't responding to her calls. Honoria and Leo were new to the area, and she'd been worried their pup would get lost. Skye had joined in the search and located him cowering in a culvert. To repay her, Honoria had invited Skye to a crawfish boil much like this one.

Skye had seen in Honoria the woman Dove might've become. Like Dove, Honoria was an artist and adored animals. They'd clicked right away.

When Jupiter scampered after a squirrel, Skye stood and took another drink, savoring the cold fizz on her parched throat. Her gaze fell on Leo, who was now mixing up their signature homemade sauce to accompany the meal. Watching him made her wonder what life would be like having Nash for a husband. The idea was both terrifying and tantalizing.

Honoria stepped in front of her, blocking her view of the patio. "Confession time. Come on. What's up?"

"Can't I want to spend time with my friend without a reason?"

"You're supposed to be glued to Nash's side. Instead, you're here acting like your world is over."

She sighed. "He asked me to marry him."

Honoria's jaw dropped. "Get out."

"He wants a marriage of convenience." She scowled. "I didn't know what that was until your mom roped me into watching that four-hour period drama."

"Get out."

"Would you stop saying that?"

She opened and closed her mouth multiple times. "You turned him down?"

"Of course I turned him down!"

"Did he have a ring? Did he get on one knee? What did he say?"

"There was no ring. It wasn't the sort of proposal you see on television. He wants a mom for Eden," she said miserably. "He's not thinking clearly. He found out he has a daughter he didn't know about, and now someone's trying to kill him." She snapped her fingers. "That's it. He's scared of leaving Eden alone in the world, and he wants someone in place to care for her."

"But she has Maeve and Virgil."

Skye bit the inside of her cheek. Virgil hadn't been cleared as a suspect. The fact that Maeve was married to the guy wouldn't reassure Nash.

Honoria's eyes brightened. "Just think…if you marry him, the four of us could go on double dates. Our kids would grow up together. I—"

"You don't have any kids."

"Not yet."

"I am not marrying him."

She folded her arms across her chest. "Is it unreasonable to think he might *actually* have feelings for you?"

Skye schooled her features, not ready to tell her friend about the kiss. "Yes."

Her feelings for Nash weren't easily defined. While Skye had dated on and off through the years, she'd avoided serious attachments. In truth, she hadn't been able to envision a future with anyone. That wasn't the case with Nash.

She had to remember why their paths had crossed in the first place. She had to keep him safe until they cracked the case. He wouldn't need her anymore after that.

"Skye—"

"How about some help over here?" Leo pointed to one of the pots and patted his belly. "My stomach's rubbin' my backbone. It's time to cook up some mudbugs."

"I'll be right there," Honoria called. She wagged her finger in Skye's face. "We're not finished." Turning on her heel, she hurried to help him lug the pot of washed crawfish and pour them into the boiling mixture.

Skye joined them, adding mushrooms, sausages and corn on the cob to the mix.

Honoria's mom and sister pulled into the driveway, and she was saved from further questions. She stayed for the meal but slipped out during a lively debate between Honoria and her sister.

Instead of heading for the ranch, Skye turned toward town. Time to switch gears. She had to get her thoughts off Nash's bombshell proposal and back to where they belonged—finding justice for Lucy before anyone else got hurt.

SIXTEEN

Nash watched Grace's rearview lights bounce over the gravel. She'd lingered over supper, drawing out the evening despite his obvious distraction. Finally, after Eden had fallen asleep, Grace had seemed to accept his reticence as a sign to leave.

He heard a clanging noise outside and noticed the door to the workshop was open and the light was on. He went to investigate and found Hardy inside.

"Thought you'd already left." His tense muscles relaxed.

"Nah. I was babysitting that new mama cow, Angel."

"And?"

"She'll do fine. Just needs some coaching is all." He gestured with the thermos. "I forgot this on your workbench. Your supper guest still hanging around?"

Nash kneaded his pounding head. "She's gone."

"That one has her eye on more than an employee position."

Nash grimaced. "You sound like Skye."

"Where is the deputy this evening?"

"I don't know."

Hardy's brow creased in silent question.

"I did something stupid."

"Wouldn't be the first time."

"I asked her to marry me."

Hardy grunted. "Why'd you go and do a thing like that?"

Because the idea had made sense in the wee hours of the night when the reality of single fatherhood had hit him. "We make a good team, Skye and me. She's good with Eden."

"That's not a reason to bring her into the family, son."

Nash couldn't keep that kiss out of his head. Although her reaction to his proposal had stung, it had been for the best. He'd thought marrying for the sake of mutual support would benefit them both. Skye and her sister would be provided for, and Eden would be raised by a strong, courageous, loving woman. Personal feelings hadn't factored into his decision. Or that was what he'd thought.

Kissing her had ripped off his blinders. He now knew that his feelings wouldn't remain docile and easily controlled. He couldn't marry a woman like Skye and remain passive and safe behind his protective walls.

She scrambled his thinking and shredded his peace. The reasons for that had altered. In the past, she'd judged him without getting to know him. As an adult, she pushed his boundaries and refused to let him stay safely in his private world.

"Why didn't you ever marry?"

Hardy's shoulders drooped. "I did."

"Why didn't I know about this? Who was she?"

Sadness was imprinted on Hardy's leathery face. "Carolyn Gilmore. We were high school sweethearts."

"What happened?"

"Got hitched right out of high school. She got pregnant right away. Nine months later, she and the baby died in childbirth."

Nash put his hand on the older man's shoulder. "I had no idea. I'm so sorry."

Hardy's Adam's apple bobbed. "No woman could hold a candle to my sweet Carolyn. I'll go to my grave loving her." He looked Nash in the eye. "If you marry Skye, do it because you can't imagine life with anyone else but her."

Nash was pondering that when an explosion rocked the ground beneath him.

"What was that?" Hardy exclaimed, the whites of his eyes showing.

Before he could answer, the metal door to the workshop slammed shut. Nash ran over and tried the knob. Tried to shoulder it open. "Won't budge."

The sound of glass breaking in the attached sales barn was followed by pinging metal on the concrete. Another explosion rocked the building, and Hardy fell to his knees. Smoke billowed into the workshop through the connecting interior door, trailed by a rush of heat that seemed to bake Nash's face.

Ears ringing, he grasped Hardy around the shoulders and helped him stand. "Call for help!"

Deputy Hank Flowers had been watching the ranch, but he'd been called away over an hour ago.

There were combustible materials in these buildings. Whoever had trapped them in here—and he had no doubt someone had—likely knew that. His heart slammed against his chest. Was that person even now going into his house to take his daughter from him?

Offering up frantic prayers, Nash quickly searched the toolboxes for something that would penetrate the exit door. Heat and smoke were advancing into the workshop. There were no windows to break through. Time was not on their side.

"They're on the way," Hardy told him. "Here!" He

found the electric drill, and the two men hurried over to try to remove the hinges. They were rusted and stubborn.

"I'm going to see if the sales-barn exits are blocked."

His face glistening with sweat, Hardy looked up at him. "Be careful, son."

Nash grabbed a cloth from the workbench and covered his mouth and nose. Hunching over, he entered the sales barn and instantly began coughing. He shifted forward, straining to see if the calf-barn doors were accessible. Flames licked along that long interior wall, greedy for the wood and hay. The fire had already spread to the roof, weakening the exposed rafters. The decades-old barn wouldn't last long at this rate.

As he neared the tractor, a deafening crack heralded the roof's collapse. Nash dived for the workshop door, reaching safety with seconds to spare. He slammed the door behind him, sucked in air and got a lungful of smoke.

Hardy threw down the drill. "Ain't gonna work."

Slowed by fits of coughing, Nash hurried through the haze to search the workbenches again. He needed something solid and heavy to knock those hinges loose. Grabbing a hammer, he returned to the door, only to find Hardy slumped over on the floor and gasping for breath.

The hammer slipped from his fingers. He crouched and shook the man's shoulder. "Hardy!"

The older man's eyes fluttered. "I'm fine. Head's just swimming."

Nash got up and banged on the door, yelling his frustration. Hardy was like a beloved uncle. He was as close to Nash as Remi was. He couldn't lose him.

How far out were the first responders? He picked up the hammer and started pounding at the hinges.

Lord, please make a way of escape.

* * *

Skye's cruiser rocketed down the darkened two-lane road, siren blaring, red and blue lights swirling through the gloom. Within minutes of leaving Honoria's house, she'd been called to assist Chen and Hank with a domestic dispute that had taken more than an hour to unravel. Then, just as she was finishing up her report, she'd heard the request for first responders to the Wilder Ranch. Her speedometer needle inched closer to ninety as her need to reach Nash and Eden squeezed the air from her lungs.

God, Honoria says that You love me and You want good for me. Help me believe it. You chose not to save my dad from that heart attack. You chose to let my mom die and my sister suffer. I'm not over that, God, but I'm begging You to step in. Please save the people I care about.

The plume of smoke and flames licking toward the star-studded sky gripped her with intense fear. Was Eden with Nash? What if she never got to see him again?

As the ranch entrance came into view, she stomped on the brake and careened beneath the arch. The cruiser bounced over the cattle guard and slung gravel far and wide. The sight of the workshop and sales barn engulfed in flames made her feel ill. Nash hadn't answered her phone calls.

Shoving her spiraling thoughts aside, she parked and hopped the fence. She contacted Dispatch and let them know she was the first on the scene. Running parallel with the untouched paddocks and larger horse barn, she headed for the workshop door. The sight that greeted her almost stopped her in her tracks. Someone had wedged a chair beneath the knob, effectively trapping whoever was inside.

A rhythmic thumping seeped through the door.

"Nash?"

Skye removed the chair, turned the knob and tugged open the door. Smoke billowed out, engulfing her. Nash's head whipped up. His face was grimy, his hair sticking to his forehead, his eyes red.

"Skye." He stared at her as if he didn't believe she was real.

Her stomach unclenched, and she reached in to seize handfuls of his shirt. "Let's go!"

He tossed a hammer to the ground. "Help me with Hardy!"

Together, they dragged the older man out and away from the building.

"Let me be," he groused, batting them away and attempting to sit up.

Nash grabbed her hand. "Eden."

The look in his eyes made her blood turn cold. Without a word, she turned and sprinted for the house. Nash was right behind her, slowed by fits of coughing. Neither one turned at the rumble of the fire truck along the driveway behind them.

Nash overtook her at the door, pushing ahead into the foyer. "Eden?"

Skye followed him down the hall and saw him shove open the bedroom door, flick on the light and barge inside. Saw him stop short, his spine going rigid.

She moved around him and stared at the empty bed.

Eden was gone.

SEVENTEEN

Skye's stomach went into free fall. Had the killer planned to abduct Eden all along? Or had he seized the opportunity once the men were trapped?

Seeing the horror on Nash's face, she thought of another option. "We don't know for sure that he has her. Was she asleep when you went outside?"

"Yes." He left the room. "The explosions could've woken her. Check all the rooms. I'll get flashlights so we can check outside."

Skye called for backup. If Eden had been startled awake and found herself alone in the house, she could've gone looking for Nash...assuming the killer hadn't taken her.

She checked under the beds, inside closets and any other spaces a frightened toddler might hide. Joining Nash in the kitchen, she noticed the patio door was ajar.

"Nash."

Again, he surged ahead, flicking on the patio light and calling Eden's name. His smoke-roughened voice vibrated with worry and hope.

Skye bent to pick up the small blanket Eden liked to sleep with. "She came this way."

He took the blanket and held it to his chest. Skye's

heart broke with his. Eden was in danger—either from the person intent on punishing Nash or from the ranch terrain itself. There were any number of risks out there.

"Call on Dax, Santi and any neighbor friends who can help us search," she told him. "Chen will contact Mayfield PD, as well as deputies from neighboring counties."

He called Santi first. After a rushed explanation, he asked the man to contact the others.

His gaze was unflinching. "We will find her."

Skye's lips wouldn't work. She couldn't lie to him, couldn't pretend everything would be okay. Life didn't always work out like that.

"Where would the killer likely access the ranch?" she said instead.

He pointed straight ahead. "There's an access road on the other side of that pasture."

"Let's go."

He left the blanket on the table and handed her one of the flashlights. He surprised her by taking her hand and uttering a quick, desperate prayer. As they left the house behind and entered the trees, she echoed the prayer.

"Which pajamas was she wearing?"

"The pink ones."

The white set would've been easier to spot in the dark. At least the weather was clear, and the temperature didn't pose a threat.

They walked far apart but in the same direction, their flashlight beams slicing through the darkness. She startled multiple birds from their roosts and stumbled over branches. When her light skimmed murky water, she gritted her teeth. This pond wasn't like the one at the entrance. Although smaller, it was covered by algae and smelled like rotting vegetation. An insect thumped her cheek, and she swatted it away.

Nash's beam bounced closer. "Let's walk the perimeter and search for footprints," he called, his urgency palpable. "I'll meet you on the opposite side."

"Got it." Her desire to surge ahead toward the access road warred with the possibility that Eden had wandered off on her own.

Skye kept her head down and eyes trained on the ground. Her shoes sank into the soft muck, letting her know that if Eden had been here, there would surely be evidence.

"I didn't see anything."

He scraped his hand down his face. "I should've ridden Rico out here. Could've covered more ground that way. Don't know what I was thinking."

"We can get the horses later. For now, let's keep going."

Nash nodded, his gaze sliding to the opaque, silent water. She didn't have to guess where his thoughts were headed.

She started walking, unwilling to let her own thoughts do the same. He followed suit. They called out for the little girl, and the answering silence became oppressive, a living, breathing monster of uncertainty.

When her light picked up a large, shifting shadow ahead, she drew her weapon and issued a command. "Stop. Police."

"Saddler?"

She adjusted the flashlight's direction and encountered Chen's annoyed face.

He pointed to the fence behind him. "No sign of anyone on this access road."

Nash quickly crossed to where they were standing. "You didn't see anything?" he demanded. "What about on your way here? No suspicious vehicles?"

Chen shook his head. "Nothing."

Skye pointed to his bleeding cheek. "What happened there?"

He lifted his fingers to the spot. "Scraped it on the fence. I'm going to continue down this road. Which direction are you going?"

Nash pinched the bridge of his nose. "Back to the house. The men should've arrived. We'll need horses and a plan."

"I'll keep you updated." Chen climbed over the fence and returned to his cruiser, only then activating the spotlight.

For the return route, they explored the property closer to the middle pasture. The more time that passed, the more tightly wound Skye became. Eden was not only a precious, innocent little girl, she was her last link to Lucy.

The patio light welcomed them. Above the roof, columns of smoke were visible.

They skirted the side of the house and encountered an active scene. Firefighters sprayed the structure with thick streams of water. Deputies from nearby counties mingled with Nash's ranch hands and neighbors willing to help. Zane and Bubba Chesterfield were not among them.

"Over here!"

Heads swiveled toward the greenhouse as the paramedic named Rachel, Grace's neighbor, emerged from the structure.

Skye gasped. "Nash!"

His breath hissed between his teeth as he half ran, half limped past the vegetable gardens. Skye stood rooted to the spot, her heart in her throat. Nash took his little girl from the paramedic and cradled her close to his chest. *This is it*, she thought. *This is the moment Nash truly becomes a father.*

Skye shook off her shock and jogged over. Eden's eyes got big when she saw her.

"Barn go boom!"

Nash lifted his head, his emotion-filled gaze locking on to hers.

Skye smoothed Eden's hair. "It sure did, sweetheart."

He looked at Rachel. "How did you find her?"

"I went over to make a phone call and heard something fall. I went inside and saw her hiding under one of the tables. She seems okay, but we should transport her to the hospital and look her over."

"I'm not letting her out of my sight." His tone brooked no argument.

"You can ride with her. You should be checked for smoke inhalation, as well," Rachel said.

Nash looked at Skye, his wishes plain.

"I'll follow the ambulance," she said, as if anyone could stop her.

Nash paused at the rear of the ambulance and glanced over at the destruction.

"How much will it cost to rebuild?" Skye asked.

"I don't care." He switched his attention to her. "You, me and Eden are safe. Hardy is okay. The enemy didn't win."

Skye's admiration for this man deepened. She hoped that was all it was.

The ambulance took them to the urgent care clinic that served Tulip and Farmdale. Nash held Eden on his lap in one of the examination rooms. She'd fallen asleep in the ambulance and hadn't stirred as he'd carried her inside. Skye had filled out the paperwork for him, and now she paced between the counter along the back wall and the door. Her curls bounced with impatience.

He could barely speak for the gratitude filling him up. Gratitude for God's mercy. Gratitude for Skye's constancy and support. Without her unwavering presence tonight, he wouldn't have been able to function.

He cleared his throat in a vain effort to dislodge the coating left over from the smoke inhalation. "About that request I made earlier…"

Skye pivoted, snagged the water bottle from the counter and held it out to him. "You mean the request that I marry you?" Her sleek brows formed a V.

He gulped the water and recapped the lid. "That would be the one."

Framing her waist with her hands, she stared at him expectantly. "What about it?"

"I didn't give it enough thought and consideration."

"You're withdrawing it, then?"

Nash couldn't decipher how she was feeling, and it was frustrating. "I spoke in haste. While I think you and I do make a great team, we probably wouldn't be content for the long haul in a relationship like that."

Something slid through her impossibly green eyes. Hurt? Regret? He hadn't set out to hurt her. She presented such a capable, can-do attitude that sometimes he forgot to consider her feelings.

"What I mean to say is—"

The door opened, and a man close to their age entered. His professional expression melted into genuine delight when he spied Skye.

"Skye, it's good to see you." His glance flicked to Nash. "I'm sorry to keep you waiting."

"Hello, Peter. We saw the waiting room. Busy night."

Skye obviously knew the doctor. Nash studied their faces as they shared bits of conversation. He wanted to know how they knew each other. If they were so familiar with each other because they'd dated. His reaction was juvenile and embarrassing. Hadn't he just told her they weren't right for each other?

Their gazes zeroed in on him. He realized they were waiting for him to answer, only he hadn't heard the question.

Peter introduced himself and bent to peer at Eden. She stirred when he took her vitals and looked her over.

"I can't find any cause for concern," he pronounced, making notes in his laptop. "I'd keep an eye on her for the next few days. Make sure she's eating and drinking. If you notice anything unusual, bring her back in."

The doctor turned his attention to Nash and checked his lungs. Thankfully, he didn't see a need to keep him overnight for observation.

Nash thanked him and stood. Now that the adrenaline had faded, his still-healing leg began to demand serious pain relief.

Peter closed his laptop and reached out to touch Skye's arm. "I hope I can see you again soon under better circumstances."

If Skye recognized the unasked question in his manner, she didn't let on. "Have a good night, Peter."

Out in the truck, which Skye had driven to the clinic, Eden continued to snooze through the process of being strapped in. Nash climbed behind the wheel but didn't immediately start the engine.

Skye looked over at him. "Are you all right? How's your leg? We should've asked Peter to check the wound."

"It's sore, that's all."

"Well, I'm exhausted and starving."

"Me, too."

"I can make—"

"Don't say it," he groaned, his lips curving involuntarily. "I don't love waffles as much as you and Eden do."

Skye softly laughed. "I'm too tired to make waffles. I was going to say I could make sandwiches when we get home."

Home. Somewhere along the way, his home now felt like Skye's. She wasn't a stranger. She was like family.

His gaze caught on her lips, where she was applying a gloss. The faint scent of strawberries wafted over. He was tempted to lean over, sink his fingers in her luxurious hair and feel her mouth beneath his again.

Get yourself together, man. You can't tell her one thing and do another. That would be unfair.

Her phone trilled. "It's Hank."

Nash listened to her side of the conversation. Once again, it seemed they were hitting a brick wall in the investigation. Finishing the call, she looked over at him.

"Bubba has an alibi. When Hank got to their ranch, Bubba was there with his friend David Dixon. David claims they were both there all evening."

He stared at the glowing red clinic letters. "Can David be trusted to tell the truth?"

"Hard to say. But listen to this. Hank spoke to the clerk at the gas station down the road from your place, and he said nothing unusual happened tonight. When Hank reviewed the security camera footage, he said he saw someone who looked like Virgil Ackerman at the pumps. He wasn't driving his registered vehicle or Maeve's, however. He was on the phone, and judging from his frantic gestures, he was having an intense conversation."

"I thought Virgil was out of town."

"Maybe that's what he wants everyone to think."

"Would you agree we have three main suspects?"

She nodded. "Virgil, Bubba and the mysterious, un-identified older man Lucy was allegedly dating."

Which one of them had killed Lucy? And which one had almost succeeded in killing him and Hardy tonight?

EIGHTEEN

The next morning, Nash and Skye walked into the Tulip library with Eden between them. Nash had watched her carefully for signs that last night's drama was troubling her. So far, the toddler was acting as if everything was normal. They figured the explosions had frightened her, and she'd slipped out the back door and around to the front, eventually making her way into the greenhouse. He reached out and smoothed her hair, his chest tightening again as he thought of the thousand ways things could've gone wrong.

He hurried to keep up with Skye, who was on a mission to locate Maeve. They wound through the stacks and around the research section, eventually reaching the conference room. The smell of tart lemons mingled with rich coffee in the wood-paneled space. About a dozen ladies were seated around the long table, with Maeve presiding at the head of it like a queen with her subjects.

Their heads swiveled at the intrusion. Maeve's eyes widened and her lips turned down. Setting her book on the table, she stood and smoothed her pink skirt.

"Skye, I thought we were supposed to meet after book club."

"Unfortunately, this can't wait. I'm sorry to interrupt, ladies, but I'll need to steal Maeve for a few minutes."

Their heads swiveled to their leader. "I suppose I could spare a few moments," she said in breathy annoyance, checking her watch. "We're short on time today. Carrie has a massage at noon, and Vera's got to pick up her grandkids from day care."

A redhead with glasses perched on the end of her nose raised her hand as if they were in class. "Do you want me to take the lead in your absence?"

Maeve's lips flattened even more. "That won't be necessary, Judy." She waved her hand over a platter of lemon squares. "Have dessert while you wait."

Eden tugged on Maeve's skirt, and the older woman's expression softened. "Hello, my sweetling. I'm happy to see you."

Her tone made it obvious Eden was the only one she was happy to see.

The four of them trooped into the hallway, and Maeve made a point to close the conference room door. Clasping her hands, she looked between them. "What is so important that couldn't wait until later?"

"We need to speak with Virgil," Skye said firmly. "He's not answering his phone. Where is he, Maeve?"

Her fingers brushed against her pearl necklace. "Why? Is he a suspect?"

"He was seen at a gas station near the ranch last night."

Maeve shot Nash a worried look. He'd phoned her after returning from the clinic and told her what had happened. He'd learned Maeve liked to keep apprised of these things. Hearing secondhand that the father of her only grandchild had had another brush with danger was not ideal.

He'd also called Remi. The ranch was hers, too, and

she deserved to know. She'd apologized once again for not being able to get time away from her cases.

"Surely you don't believe Virgil would hurt anyone? He may come across as brusque, but he's actually a big softy. You don't know him like I do. Besides, he's in Nevada. See?" She pulled out her phone and showed them a photo of the Las Vegas strip. "He texted this to me yesterday."

"You do realize that doesn't prove his whereabouts. Not until experts examine his phone. What's the name of his hotel?"

"He's staying in a vacation rental house." Maeve's expression turned stormy. "Are you fixated on my husband because you don't have any other viable suspects?"

"I'm following leads, Maeve. That's my job, no matter how uncomfortable that may make you."

"If there are no other questions, I need to get back in there."

Skye gestured for her to go ahead. After patting Eden on the head, she went inside and closed the door.

Skye sighed. "I'll contact the rental owners. If they don't have security cameras or haven't actually seen Virgil, we can't verify he was there. I doubt the judge will give us a warrant on Virgil's or Maeve's phone at this point."

They returned to the ranch, and Nash's gaze raked over the smoldering ruins. Yellow police tape roped off the area. Arson investigators would look into the cause of the fire. The explosions he and Hardy had heard suggested the use of homemade explosive devices.

He felt oddly dispassionate about the loss of equipment and property. If his father were here, he'd be raving and ranting and promising retribution. But Nash's close brush with death—and the fear he'd lost Eden—had reminded

Nash what truly mattered. It wasn't proving something to his father or grandfather or previous Wilders that he deserved to possess this land.

I'm sorry, God, for losing sight of why I'm here...to live like the Bible teaches. To love You first and my neighbor as myself.

As they got closer to the house, they noticed a late-model gold sedan parked beside Grace's Jeep. Grace herself was ensconced in one of the rocking chairs, and she was speaking to a woman with short black hair.

Skye shot him an inquisitive glance.

"I forgot the vet was coming out today to vaccinate the horses," he said.

"Why is Grace hanging around your front stoop?" she asked lightly.

"She must've heard about the fire and wondered if she should open the store today as planned."

When Nash and Skye emerged from the truck, both Grace and Leslie joined them in the driveway. Grace came up to Nash, grasped his biceps and stared up at him.

"Nash, I'm so sorry. I had no idea you were in danger. If only I'd stuck around a little longer, I could've prevented this."

Her proximity made him nervous, especially with Skye looking on. "It's not your fault," he reassured her. Sidestepping Grace, he greeted Leslie.

A furrow deepened between the vet's brows as she took in the damage. "I just learned about the fire when I arrived. Are any of your animals in need of attention?"

"No, and I'm grateful for that."

"You're one blessed man," she said fervently.

He had to agree. God had blessed him in so many ways.

"Do you know who was behind it?" Grace interjected.

"We have our theories," Skye said, carrying Eden around the hood. "You said you were here last night, Grace?"

Her eyes pinched. "Remember, I brought chili to share?" She reached out to Eden, who went willingly into her arms.

"You didn't see anything unusual as you were leaving?" Skye asked.

"Nothing, I'm afraid."

Leslie cleared her throat. "Nash, can I speak to you for a moment?"

"Sure."

"It's about Lucy."

"Then Skye should be included in the conversation."

The three of them walked closer to the workshop.

"There's been a lot of speculation surrounding Lucy's murder," Leslie said. "I've been following the news reports, and I remembered something that might be important."

"What is it?" Skye asked.

She held up her hand in caution. "I debated whether or not to even mention it, because I don't know if it will be useful or just another distraction. I'm certainly not accusing this man of a crime." She licked her lips. "About three months ago, I was called out to a ranch on the far side of Farmdale. I stopped off at a truck stop for a quick bite, and I saw Lucy Ackerman having supper with Zane Chesterfield."

Nash worked to contain his surprise. Why had Zane and Lucy been together? And why hadn't Zane mentioned it? Could he possibly be the mysterious love interest?

Skye wanted to go back to the Chesterfield Ranch and pursue the vet's information. Nash turned down Grace's offer to watch Eden, and Skye was relieved. She still wasn't over the fright she'd received last night. She felt better having the little girl within sight.

Zane wasn't at his ranch. One of his ranch hands said the men were at the farmers' co-op, so Skye and Nash headed there with Eden in tow. The co-op wasn't busy. They walked through the interior space and exited into the fenced-in outdoor area where they housed the plants, fertilizer and assorted mulches. Zane and Bubba were inspecting galvanized steel tubs.

"What do you want now?" Bubba growled, throwing up his hands. "Haven't you stained our good name enough? Do you have to hunt us down in public?"

Zane put a restraining hand on Bubba's arm.

"We have questions…" Skye began.

"Always more questions," Bubba griped. "You're unable to find the culprit, so you keep coming back to me."

"Actually, I'm here for Zane."

Bubba's features contorted. "What does my father have to do with Lucy?"

Zane dropped his hand, and the color drained from his face.

"You might as well tell me everything," Skye advised. "We have a witness."

"What's she talking about, Dad?" Bubba demanded.

Running his fingers through his hair, Zane hefted a heavy sigh. "I didn't want you to find out this way, son. I know you cared for her as more than a friend—"

"Find out what? What's going on?"

Zane kept his silence, so Skye filled Bubba in. "Someone saw Zane and Lucy having supper about three months ago."

"She never told me," Bubba said, his brows crashing together. "Did you meet to talk about me?"

Nash grunted. "I'm sure they talked about you, but probably not in the way you think."

Zane looked resigned. "Lucy and I were sweet on each other."

Bubba laughed outright. "Sure."

"Lucy told you she was dating an older man," Nash reminded him. "She was talking about your father."

Bubba's hands opened and closed. "I don't believe it."

"Son, we didn't want to hurt your feelings. That's why we kept our relationship a secret. I loved her. I wanted to marry her, but she hemmed and hawed. Said it would cause too many problems with folks in Tulip."

Bubba shook his head, obviously having a hard time accepting this revelation. "You're old enough to be her father!"

"Age wasn't an issue between us," Zane replied quietly.

Bubba stormed off, ignoring his father's request to come back.

Zane looked at Nash. "I'm sorry I didn't tell you about Eden. I tried to convince Lucy to come clean. She could be stubborn about some things, and she insisted you weren't interested in being a dad."

Nash turned ashen. Skye rested her hand on his lower back.

He held Eden closer. "She couldn't have been more wrong."

Zane nodded somberly. "I can see that." To Skye, he said, "I loved Lucy. I would've given her the world, if I could."

"You'll have to come down to the station for formal questioning," Skye informed him. "We'll need alibis for the time of Lucy's death, as well as the attacks against Nash and me."

"I understand."

The seasoned rancher projected a humble regret that hinted at his innocence. However, a person with a lot to lose could be a convincing actor when he needed to be. He'd allowed his own son to be considered a suspect, and that didn't sit well with her.

The clouds overhead began spitting rain as they made their way through the exit and to their vehicles. While Nash got Eden settled in his truck, Skye hustled Zane into the rear seat of her cruiser.

She paused in the open driver's door and looked across the car roof. "It may be a while before I get done," she told Nash.

He tipped up his Stetson. "I'm sticking close to the house today. I'm gonna grill chicken for lunch. Want me to save you some?"

It struck her how familiar they'd become with each other. "I'd like that."

The rain unleashed in earnest, ending their conversation.

Chen was waiting for them at the station. After instructing Skye to take notes, he jumped right into the interrogation. Zane supplied his whereabouts during the murder and subsequent attacks, as well as names of those who could corroborate his accounts. The only time he lost his temper was when Chen insinuated that Bubba had found out about Zane and Lucy's relationship and had killed her in retaliation. After all, he must've felt betrayed.

Skye had seen Bubba's reaction firsthand. It had seemed authentic. "Why let him take the heat in this case?"

Zane's face flushed, his eyes sparking. "Because I knew he was innocent and that nothing would come of it."

"You're convinced of his innocence because you're

the one who killed her?" Chen pressed. "Or maybe the two of you were in on it together?"

"No." The vein in his temple bulged. "You're grasping at straws. I want a lawyer."

Chen huffed in annoyance and flicked his fingers at her. "Put him in the holding cell and follow up on those names he gave us."

As Skye was locking the cell door behind Zane, he sent her an imploring look. "Do me a favor? Check on my boy. He's upset, and I don't want him to do anything rash."

"What do you think he might do, Zane?"

"That's the thing. I don't know."

Skye stared into his eyes. Was he the murderer? Or was that person still walking around free?

NINETEEN

Droplets of water dripped off Nash's hat and splashed onto his slicker. The rain had started yesterday morning as they'd left the co-op and hadn't let up. More than twenty-four hours later, the ground had turned into a soggy mess. That made untangling this cow from the fencing she'd tried to jump even harder than usual. Why she'd wandered off from the herd late at night was anyone's guess.

"Shine the light where I can see what I'm doing," he reminded Dax, who'd been vocal in his wish to be anywhere but on the ranch.

Santi sat astride his horse, ready to direct the heifer where they wanted once she was free. "Is she injured?"

"I can't tell yet," Nash answered.

"Would serve her right," Dax griped. "I had to cancel a supper date, thanks to this heifer's shenanigans."

Nash ignored him. "Hardy, hold her legs."

Hardy held her down while Nash snipped the wire and got out of her way. Instead of heading for the barn and dry hay, she hurtled through the opening in the fence, this time crossing over onto Chesterfield land.

Dax slapped his thigh and vocalized his frustration in ear-burning vocabulary.

Hardy scrambled after her. She sped up, mooing her displeasure. Or was she laughing at them? Nash ran after Hardy, nearly skidding into him when the man stopped on a dime.

"Why'd you stub up like that? I almost knocked you into the next pasture."

"My boot struck something. Dax, bring that flashlight."

Muttering, Dax stomped over. "We're letting that girl get away. Zane and Bubba aren't gonna be happy."

Santi directed the beam to the ground at their feet.

Nash's blood ran cold. "Are my eyes playing tricks on me?"

Hardy crouched for a closer look, and Nash followed suit. Neither one spoke for long moments.

"I'm lookin' at a human hand," Hardy finally said. "Is that what you're lookin' at?"

Nash grunted, his gaze fixated on the limp hand poking out of the mud. Dread skittered down his spine.

Dax walked closer and let out a disbelieving gurgle.

Nash pushed to his feet. "Santi, call the police. Tell them we've discovered a dead body."

He walked away from the others and called Skye. When Hardy had called about the wayward cow, she had been feeding Eden supper.

"Did you rescue the heifer?" Skye said in greeting. "Eden and I made brownies, enough to share with the guys. She's already had her bath. We're watching her favorite show, and we're having trouble staying awake."

He closed his eyes, easily picturing the alluring deputy and his daughter together on his couch.

"Skye, we've made a discovery. I'm going to send Hardy to the house to stay with Eden. I'll need you to ride one of the four-wheelers out here. He'll give you directions."

"What sort of discovery?" Her voice switched to cop mode.

He rubbed his forehead. "A dead body. I think it's a male, based on the hand size, but I can't be sure."

"On your land?"

"No, just across the property line on the Chesterfields'. Santi is already in touch with Dispatch."

"Don't let anyone disturb the scene."

"Yes, ma'am."

The rain continued to lightly splatter everything within sight. Skye arrived on the four-wheeler ahead of any other law enforcement. She wore her police rain slicker with the hood pulled up to protect her hair and face. She parked so that the headlamps lit up the break in the fence and then slogged through the wet earth to get to him.

"The Mayfield CSU is on their way. Could be an hour or more before they get here." She peered past him. "Show me what you found."

Dax was on his phone farther down the fence line, no doubt talking to one of his many lady friends. Santi remained astride his horse, somber and quiet.

Nash assisted her over the tangle of wire. She crouched and inspected the area with her gaze.

"Looks like the soil has been disturbed recently. We'll be able to see more once the spotlights are set up."

"I tried calling Bubba and Zane. Neither one is picking up. I left them messages to call me ASAP."

The sheriff's department hadn't had enough to hold Zane, so they'd released him yesterday after his lawyer showed up.

She stood and swiped the raindrops from her cheek. "Whoever put this body here didn't check the forecast."

"Do you think Sheriff Hines will cut his vacation short once he hears?"

"It's very likely." She pulled out her phone. "I'm going to text Hank and ask him to swing by the Chesterfield house."

Nash glanced at the exposed hand, wondering who this person might be and praying for their family members who would soon learn gruesome news.

Once Chen and the CSU arrived, Skye and Nash moved out of the way. Dax and Santi gave their statements and left. Nash's stray cow would be run down at first light. Identifying the body was first priority.

He wasn't sure how much time passed as the unit processed the scene and finally began to unearth the victim. Chen remained near the site, watching the proceedings like a hawk. When he waved them over, Nash's muscles tensed.

"Who is it?" Skye asked, striding beside him.

"See for yourself," he retorted. "I've got to report this to Sheriff Hines." Stomping off, he began to speak tersely into the phone.

Skye and Nash peered into the grave, now protected from the elements by a canopy and illuminated by the powerful lights. He started when her fingers threaded through his and clutched tightly.

"I guess he wasn't out of town after all."

Nash stared at the lifeless body of Virgil Ackerman. Like Lucy, he'd been stabbed multiple times in the chest.

Who would kill Virgil and stash him here? Either the killer had done a poor job of burying him, or he hadn't cared if Virgil was unearthed.

Skye's phone rang, causing her to flinch. Pulling her fingers free, she answered it. "Hank, did you talk to them?" She looked over at Nash and ended the call. "No one answered the door, and both Zane's and Bubba's vehicles are gone."

"What would they gain from killing Virgil? And why bury him on their own land?"

"More questions I don't know the answers to," she said, her jaw tense. Her green eyes were stark. "Nash, how am I going to tell Maeve?"

Sergeant Chen took center stage the following morning at an impromptu town meeting. Sheriff Hines was on his way back to Tulip and had instructed Chen to address the citizens' concerns without compromising the investigation. From her angle on the church's platform, Skye could see his grip on the podium and the stiffness of his stance. People had crowded into the sanctuary and were lobbing questions left and right. Skye was glad she didn't have to field them. She was still emotionally drained from her visit with Maeve the previous night.

Nash had remained at the house with Eden while Hank had accompanied Skye to the Ackerman residence. With Chen and other law enforcement roaming the Chesterfield land so close to the Wilder Ranch, Skye had felt safe enough leaving them alone.

Maeve had promptly fainted upon hearing of Virgil's death, and Skye and Hank had summoned an ambulance. Maeve had ultimately refused a trip to the hospital, but she'd cut their visit short to grieve in privacy. Her presence here this morning was unexpected.

Draped in head-to-toe black, a wide-brimmed hat shading her wan features, she sat on the front pew surrounded by her closest supporters—a black rose in the midst of a bed of spring blooms.

Nash and his crew stood along the back wall. Morning light filtering through stained glass fell across him and Eden, painting their faces in shades of pink, yellow and green.

"I'll take one final question," Chen said, shifting his stance.

"Are you going to cancel the Magnolia Festival?"

Gasps and murmurs rippled through the crowd. People started debating the pros and cons of canceling their town's annual spring event. Chen glanced back at Skye, brows raised. They hadn't discussed how to proceed. In truth, the event had slipped her mind.

The festival would begin with a kickoff concert tomorrow night, and a slew of events slated for the rest of the weekend would follow. Months of preparation went into the Magnolia Festival. People from Tulip and surrounding towns brought flowers, vegetables and fruits to sell. Craft vendors and artists brought out their wares. There were contests ranging from the best homemade jam to a floral design competition.

When Skye shrugged, Chen scowled and turned back to the crowd. He held up his hand and demanded silence. "The deputies and I will discuss the matter and make a decision today."

"Sergeant Chen?" A wobbly voice echoed through the space. All eyes focused on Maeve as she rose. "If I may say a word?"

He sighed. "Go ahead, Mrs. Ackerman."

She held a crumpled lace handkerchief in her hands. Her eyes were barely visible beneath the brim of her hat. Her lips were devoid of their usual bold color, making her look frail.

"I would like to request that the festival continue as scheduled. The festival committee members and I have been planning this since the end of last year's event. We've worked countless hours lining up musical groups and food vendors, obtaining permits, renting out spaces for the crafters and growers, prepping the judges for the many contests. This event brings in people from across southern Mississippi, and the economic impact for our citizens cannot be overstated. Our town has seen terrible days in recent weeks. I've suffered losses no one woman should have to endure." She paused. "Please don't add to these tragedies by taking away the one thing that will boost our morale."

The crowd started clapping, and the sound bounced off the rafters as Maeve resumed her seat.

When the noise finally died down, Chen again spoke. "Thank you, Mrs. Ackerman. In order to proceed as planned, we will have to find a way to balance our town's safety with the festival's many benefits."

An older cowboy ambled to his feet. "I volunteer to patrol on Saturday!"

The man next to him stood. "I'm in." He gestured around him. "Who else will join us and defend our town?"

Skye locked gazes with Nash, who rightly looked concerned. Before long, more than two dozen men had volunteered to shore up the police presence. Chen again had to control the outbursts, thanking them for their offers and reiterating that Sheriff Hines would have the final say.

When the sanctuary had almost been cleared, Nash and Eden walked to the front, where she, Chen and Hank had congregated. Eden held out her arms for Skye, her big blue eyes bright and smile as sweet as maple syrup. Skye hugged her close. She smelled like sunshine and baby and a hint of syrup, probably because she'd gotten some on her shirt at breakfast. Her heart ached at the thought of leaving Eden once this case was solved.

Lifting her glance, she got lost in Nash's electric blue eyes. How was she supposed to walk away from him and live in the same town? She supposed they could meet up from time to time so she could see Eden, but would that be fair to the little girl? A day or two a month wouldn't be nearly enough with father or daughter.

"What's your take on the festival?" he asked.

"Zane and Bubba are being held at the station. I think a lot of people feel like that means the danger has passed."

They'd eventually located the Chesterfield men in the next county over. They'd been helping out a friend and had acted shocked when confronted about Virgil's murder. Because of their involvement with Lucy, both were being held temporarily while the investigation continued.

Nash crossed his arms. "But you're not convinced?"

"Are you?"

"I don't know what to think."

"I want justice for Lucy and Virgil, and I aim to get it, no matter how long it takes."

"Maeve deserves to have closure," he said. "I offered to bring Eden over later, but she said she has funeral arrangements to tend to on top of last-minute festival details."

"At least she has support. Her friends will help lighten the load."

She shifted Eden to her other hip. "Listen, Nash, things might change once Sheriff Hines returns."

He cocked his head. "How so?"

"He might put an end to your protection detail."

He took a moment to absorb the implications. "I see."

Skye wished she could read his thoughts. Her heart felt like it was ripping in two. Did their eventual parting bother him at all?

"Let's get back to the ranch," he said. "I'm meeting the insurance adjuster in an hour."

"And I'm going to check in with the officer standing guard over the burial site."

The CSU team had removed Virgil's body, but had left an officer in place in case they needed to conduct further analysis at the site.

An unfamiliar truck sat in the ranch's driveway. It was a late model with out-of-state tags. The body was gray with silver and purple accents.

"Is that the adjuster?" Skye asked.

Nash shook his head. "He's early if it is."

They parked alongside the truck. Skye was lowering Eden to her feet when the house door flew open, and a brunette tornado whirled into the yard headed straight for Nash. She leaped into his arms, and he stumbled backward, bumping into the driver's-side door. Skye put a protective hand out for Eden while simultaneously reaching for her weapon. The woman stepped back, her mouth curved in unbridled joy.

Nash gaped at her. "Remi, what are you doing here?"

TWENTY

"What have you done to yourself?" Nash tweaked a lock of his sister's stick-straight hair, which had been dyed dark brown and lopped off just below her chin.

"I've been involved in an undercover gig," she said, shrugging. "Thought I'd go all in this time."

He looked her over, thinking she looked thinner than usual. Her blue eyes held new shadows that hadn't been there before. He worried about her being in law enforcement, especially working the narcotics unit in Atlanta.

Skye walked around the truck, holding Eden's hand. "Hello, Remi. It's good to see you."

Remi's smile was genuine. "Skye, it's been years." When she spotted Eden, her eyes got huge. She pressed her palms together. "Oh, Nash, look at her!"

Crouching, she grinned at Eden. "I'm your aunt Remi. I'm so happy to meet you."

A lump formed in his chest. He was happy that Remi was here. He wished with all his heart that his mom could meet his daughter, too.

Eden pressed against Skye's leg. Remi cocked her head to peer up at Skye. "Nash told me you've been a huge help with her. Thank you."

Skye's expression revealed deep fondness for Eden. "It hasn't been a burden."

Nash's heart flipped over. *Lord, please don't let the sheriff take her off the case. I need her with me, and so does Eden.*

He didn't want to think about not seeing Skye every day. Of seeing her on patrol on occasion and acting like they hadn't shared anything special.

"I'll leave you two to catch up." Skye motioned behind her. "I've got to check in at the site."

He nodded and reached out his hand to Eden. "See you in a bit. I'll fix coffee for everyone."

"Thanks."

She climbed onto a four-wheeler and took off, the sun glinting on her hair.

"Where's she going?" Remi asked, brow creased.

"Let's go inside. I'll fill you in before the adjuster gets here."

The air-conditioned interior was a welcome contrast to the humid afternoon, and he headed straight for the kitchen. Eden clung to his hand, sneaking glances at Remi, who slid onto a bar stool and watched him bustle about.

After placing cookies on a plate and pouring milk for Eden into her sippy cup, he lifted her onto the stool beside his sister's.

He set a cup of coffee in front of Remi, poured one for himself and leaned against the opposite counter. He relayed everything that had happened since Skye had found Lucy.

She hefted a sigh. "Never thought this would happen in Tulip."

"It's been the most trying time of my life." He looked over at Eden, who was quietly nibbling on her cookies, her gaze sliding repeatedly to Remi. "It's also been the most rewarding."

"I can't believe you're a father." Remi's lips curved as she regarded Eden. "While she has your eyes and chin, she favors Lucy."

A familiar sadness gripped him. Choices he couldn't undo haunted him. The one thing he didn't regret was Eden. Never that. "I wish she'd trusted me. She might still be alive today."

"It wasn't right to deprive you of your daughter." Remi's voice roughened. "I'll never understand how she could doubt you."

"I guess I got too good at throwing up walls. Back in high school, Lucy complained that I didn't let her in. She must've felt that nothing had changed."

"That's not an excuse."

"God's helping me work through my anger. She's not here to defend her choices, after all."

"Eden seems taken with Skye."

"Oh, she is."

"Are you?"

He stiffened. "Why do you ask?"

"Still throwing up walls, I see." She smirked. "I didn't detect the same hostility that used to exist between you. In fact, I picked up a vibe."

"In the five minutes we were all together?" He snorted, trying to deflect her attention. "She's here on orders from her superior. Speaking of law enforcement, how many days off did they give you?"

"I'm here for a week. More, if you need me."

"Good. You'll have time to bond with Eden. You have to promise to stay out of harm's way. Tulip isn't the safest place to be right now. Patrick couldn't come with you?"

"Patrick and I split up." She ducked her head over her cup, taking a long sip.

Nash set his cup down with a thunk. "When?"

Patrick was the reason she'd moved to Atlanta. They'd seemed solid, and Nash had assumed they'd eventually get married.

"A year ago."

"A year? Why didn't you say anything?"

Her gaze slid away but not before he saw the unhappiness there. He had the urge to call up Patrick and give him a piece of his mind.

"I've been busy with cases."

"Are you going to stay in Atlanta?"

"I've made a life for myself there. I have the respect of my fellow officers. I have friends. A church."

"You have a home here," he reminded her. "And now a niece who needs to know her aunt."

Eden chose that moment to offer Remi a cookie.

Chuckling, Remi accepted it and took a big bite. "Mmm. Thank you, Eden."

Nash would love to have Remi back in Tulip, but he also wanted her to be happy. He made a mental note to pray about the matter.

The insurance adjuster arrived, and they accompanied him out to the workshop and sales barn. Remi wore a troubled expression as she walked with them, listening to Nash and the man discuss the damage and process of rebuilding. When he'd gone, she punched him in the arm.

"You glossed over how bad the fire was," she accused.

"Skye rescued us." With minutes to spare, he reckoned.

The hum of the four-wheeler greeted them, and they paused to wait for Skye.

"Any developments?" he asked.

"I'm afraid not."

Eden skipped over to her. "Waffles?"

Skye chuckled and ruffled her hair. "Maybe."

At Remi's questioning look, Nash said, "Skye's obsession with waffles has transferred to Eden."

"I'll let Skye tell me the details about this obsession of hers, as well as everything that has happened since all the trouble started."

Skye glanced between them.

Nash frowned. "I already told you."

"I want to hear it from her."

"Why?"

"Because she won't sugarcoat anything. She'll shoot it to me straight."

Nash looked at Skye, silently imploring her not to mention the ill-advised marriage proposal. Remi's reaction would be tough to deal with. She'd either tease him mercilessly or try to talk him into doing it again...for real this time.

The following morning, Skye served her favorite waffles...thick golden batter studded with toasted pecans, drizzled with syrup and sprinkled with powdered sugar. She topped them off with a generous mound of whipped cream.

Perched on her preferred chair, Eden gleefully bounced on her knees and wasted no time forking one of the small bites.

Remi took a big whiff and moaned. "You're going to spoil me." She waved her fork in the direction of the kitchen. "I'm doing the dishes."

"I won't argue with that. I prefer to do the cooking and not the cleanup."

After placing fresh berries in the middle of the table, Skye retrieved her plate and sat beside Eden. That put her directly across from Nash's sister. They hadn't spent much time around each other during their school days. Skye remembered her as a popular, bright, bubbly girl— very different from her reserved, enigmatic older brother. Remi had retained her friendly manner, but Skye sensed life experience had dulled her optimism. Law enforcement could do that to a person.

True to her word, Remi had commandeered Skye last night, led her out to the horse barn and peppered her with questions. Skye hadn't needed to see the look of panic in Nash's eyes to know not to mention their marriage-of-convenience conversation. Remi had kept the questions related to the case, anyway, which spoke of her professionalism.

Skye liked the woman, and she enjoyed the siblings' interactions. Remi often teased Nash, whose grumbling was clearly a matter of show. Their obvious affection and respect for one another was a bittersweet reminder of what Skye was missing with her own sister.

Halfway through breakfast, Nash entered the house. After a quick stop at the utility room sink, he strode inside looking like the cover model for *Western Horseman*. He tweaked Remi's hair on his way around the table and bent to kiss Eden's cheek. Straightening, his electric blue gaze fell on Skye, and he paused, his focus drifting to her mouth.

The memory of the kiss surged, accompanied by the delightfully dangerous sensations it had created inside her. The moment stretched awkwardly, broken only by Remi's dramatic throat clearing. Nash dragged his gaze away, snatched a strawberry and popped it into his mouth.

"Are you going to stand there all morning mooning at Skye, or do you plan to join us?" Remi said, her smile stretching from ear to ear.

The tips of his ears turned red, and he pivoted to the kitchen. "I was planning on taking breakfast to go. I've finally been given the go-ahead to repair the fence." He slathered syrup and cream on one waffle and topped it with a second before taking a generous bite.

"CSU is finished out there?" Skye asked.

He wrapped the waffle sandwich in a paper towel. "Yes, ma'am."

"I have to be at the festival at five," she reminded him. The concert started at seven, but people would start trickling in early to set up their picnic blankets and chairs.

"I don't know if I feel comfortable having Eden there."

Remi twisted in her seat. "I'll stay here with her."

"Are you sure?"

Skye lowered her fork. "Why don't all three of you stay here?"

He finally looked her full in the face, his brows crashing together. "It's not safe for you to go alone. Remember what happened at the rodeo."

"I'm required to be there. You're not." She felt confident that between Remi's experience and Nash's military training, they could handle themselves here on the ranch.

"I am required to be there because you need protecting as much as me. I'm going, and that's that."

His stance dared her to challenge him. His determination to protect her made her feel cherished.

"Fine."

"Fine."

When he'd gone, Remi didn't try to hide her amusement. "Well."

Skye ducked her head and tucked into her breakfast, relieved when Remi didn't launch an interrogation.

They spent the day entertaining Eden. Nash returned

to the house in time to shower and change. On their drive to the festival site, he broke the silence.

"I want to thank you again for everything you've done for us," he said earnestly. "I hope having Remi around hasn't made things awkward."

"Remi is great. I've enjoyed spending time with her."

"Glad to hear it."

"How long has it been since she's been home?"

"Over a year. I flew out to see her this past Christmas."

"Did she also have a difficult relationship with your father?"

His hands flexed on the wheel. "Wes didn't hold her to the same standards as he did me. However, he was disconnected emotionally."

Skye mulled that over. No wonder talk of feelings made Nash uncomfortable. It also explained why he would consider a marriage of convenience an agreeable choice. There was no risk in it.

What a pair they made. She craved love and connection. He was determined to avoid it. Neither one felt deserving or worthy.

"Do you think Remi will ever move home?"

"I don't know."

She detected a hint of worry. The festival site came into view before she could pose a follow-up question.

He let out a low whistle. "I wondered if our recent troubles would keep the attendance down."

"Looks to be the same as last year."

He parked in the grass overflow lot, and they walked together toward the concert area. Skye imagined taking his hand and tucking closer to his side. What would it feel like to be a real couple? To be Nash's girlfriend? His wife?

Her heart stuttered in her chest. If she'd said yes to his proposal, she'd be planning their wedding.

She stumbled, and Nash quickly caught her. "Whoa, there. You okay?"

His face was so close. She rested her hand on his chest and felt his heart galloping away.

"Skye, I—"

"Deputy Saddler."

Startled, they broke apart, and Skye found herself staring at her stern-faced sheriff. Standing slightly off to the side was a smirking Sergeant Chen.

"Sheriff Hines." She wiped her damp palms on her pants. "I didn't realize you'd gotten home. How was your trip?"

Sweat gleamed on his ruddy face. His piercing gaze slid between them. "Chen informed me of your arrangement with Mr. Wilder. That's over. We've got the Chesterfield men in custody, and we can no longer spare county resources on private bodyguard duty."

Her heart sank. Not only did this mean the end of her time with Nash, but she wasn't convinced of Zane's or Bubba's guilt. "But, sir—"

"I heard about your eviction. You and I will have a sit-down after the festival. For now, I want you patrolling the crowd."

She bit the inside of her cheek. "Yes, sir."

He marched off, Chen shooting her a gloating look before following in his wake.

Nash's fingers skimmed her back. "Why did he act like this assignment was your doing?"

"Chen no doubt insinuated I asked for it." Frustration burned inside her. "He's putting you and Eden at risk, and I don't like it. We don't know for sure if we have the murderer in custody."

He put his hand on her shoulder and gently urged her around. "We're going to be okay."

She couldn't mask her unease. "You can't know that."

"God has protected us so far, hasn't He?"

"I want to trust Him."

"He's worthy of your trust."

She nodded, fighting waves of emotion. The reality of leaving the ranch hit her hard. "I'll pack my things tonight."

"Wait until after the festival." He lowered his hand to his side, his expression resigned. "Where will you go?"

"Honoria's offered to let me crash there until I make a plan."

Her future looked bleaker than it had when she'd first glimpsed that eviction notice. She'd tasted the sweetness of family life, and she wasn't ready to give it up.

TWENTY-ONE

Nash's plan to go to the festival that day went sideways, thanks to his cows. Ranch life sometimes threw curveballs, and he had to put out fires—figurative and literal. Somehow, a gate had been left open, and a hundred head of cattle had flooded the roadway. He, Hardy and Santi worked all morning to round up every last one. They could've used Dax's help, but he was at home with his ailing mother.

Skye's absence weighed on him. She'd left early that morning for the festival, and she hadn't even taken the time to make waffles. He'd had a quick breakfast of toast and jam while the waffle maker sat cold and unused on the counter. She'd take it with her when she left tomorrow night. How quickly he'd gotten used to having her around.

Brushing the dust from his jeans, he entered the ranch's store in search of Remi and Eden. Grace's car was the only one in the gravel lot outside. She was leaning over the register, her chin in her palm. Remi stood on the opposite side of the counter, holding Eden in her arms and swaying side to side. Eden's droopy eyes perked up at the sight of him as she lifted her head.

"Afternoon, ladies." His fingers skimmed the tomatoes

and cucumbers as he passed the wooden bins. "How's it going?"

Remi beamed at him. "She's decided I'm trustworthy, it seems."

He smiled and smoothed Eden's baby-fine hair, glad the shadows seemed to be banished from his sister's eyes. He hoped they didn't return.

Grace cleared her throat, her expression solemn. "We've only had three customers today, and that was before ten a.m. Would you mind if I close up early and go to the festival?"

"Sure. I'll lock up."

"Thanks. Talk to you later, Remi."

"'Bye, Grace."

She beat a hasty retreat, the hinges squeaking as the door swung closed behind her. Eden wriggled down and went to retrieve one of her toys in the corner.

Nash rubbed his jaw. "Grace doesn't seem her usual chipper self."

Remi propped one hand on her hip. "She confided that she has a crush on you. I told her it's a lost cause because there's something going on between you and Skye."

His shoulders tightened. "Skye told you about the proposal? I didn't think she would."

"Whoa." Remi's eyes widened. "What proposal?"

Nash gritted his teeth.

Remi closed in, thumping him in the stomach. "Spill it, big brother."

"It hardly matters now. She turned me down, and then I withdrew it."

"Are you kidding me?" Her eyes narrowed. "She rejected you, and instead of fighting for her, you said you didn't mean it in the first place? If there was a romance boot camp, I'd put you on the first bus, Nash Wilder."

He rubbed his hands down his face. "It wasn't romantic, okay?"

"I don't understand."

"She's great with Eden."

Remi gasped.

"She also needs a place to live."

Shaking her head, she groaned. "My brother, the clueless cowboy."

"People get married for a lot of reasons other than love," he grumbled.

"Really? What people, Nash?"

He clamped his lips together.

"Can you honestly tell me you don't care for her? Because it didn't take me long to figure out she cares about you...despite your thick head."

Could she be right? Could Skye have feelings for him? His heart danced around the idea, hopeful but scared. She deserved the best, and he wasn't sure he was her best option.

Remi waved her hand in front of his face, drawing him back to the present. "If you've found someone you can't live without, you can't just give up. Go after her."

Her words were reminiscent of Hardy's. Nash kept coming back to what his old friend had said, and he couldn't imagine sharing his life with anyone other than Skye.

"I'm going to the festival."

Her smile reminded him of his mom, and he hugged her. "I love you, sis."

He left before she got mushy on him.

At the festival, he searched the crowds for Skye, eventually seeing her at the flower booths. He recognized the cowboy at her side and frowned. Dax was supposed to be at home, caring for his mom.

Before he could start their way, he was stopped by another rancher. When he looked up again, she was gone.

Skye walked with Dax to a basket-weaving booth. He'd asked for her help in choosing a gift for his mom. She agreed to the unusual request because he was Nash's employee. Plus, he'd had an earnest look in his eyes, like he really wanted to please his mother. It was hard to overlook that kind of devotion.

He pointed out the ones he thought she might like, and Skye offered her opinions.

"Thanks, Deputy." He paid for his purchase and waited for the seller to wrap it in paper. "You know, it's a shame you won't be around the ranch anymore."

Skye didn't want to think about the lonely days ahead. Already, she missed Nash and Eden.

He accepted the wrapped package, and they strolled past vendors and dodged children darting through the throng. Up ahead, the lemonade stand beckoned to her. Her feet hurt from standing all day, and her stomach was unhappy about missing lunch.

Skye spotted Chen near the children's inflatables. He was engaged in a heated conversation with a man she didn't recognize. She slowed, not in the mood for his condescending attitude.

"Dax, I'm going to find something to eat."

He tugged the brim of his Stetson and flashed his pearly whites. "Thanks for your advice, Deputy."

Nodding, she turned and retraced her steps. The flower booths were located on the left edge of the festival site, flowing around the former mercantile that was now a rental space. Judy, the redhead from Maeve's book club, waved her over.

Skye crossed through the flow of people to get to the booth she was manning.

"Deputy Saddler, I was just about to come looking for you. I'm worried about Maeve. She's clearly exhausted. I've never seen her so overwrought before, but she refuses to go home. Says there's nothing for her there." Her brow knitted. "She mentioned speaking to you would make her feel better."

Skye wasn't so sure about that, but she agreed to try. Maybe Maeve thought she had more information about the case. "Where is she?"

"I'll show you."

Walking between booths, she followed Judy into the mercantile, breathing in the faint scent of furniture polish. This first-floor space was massive, with exposed brick walls, round tables, a bar and a stage in the rear. Far above, the ceiling was comprised of painted wooden slats, the electric wires exposed. The light streaming through the plate-glass windows only reached about a fourth of the way in. Near the stage, three women were cloaked by shadows. Maeve, seated on a lone bench, was flanked by two of her closest friends.

"I think Maeve needs a doctor," the brunette stated.

Maeve dabbed her cheeks with her handkerchief. "I'm fine, Nadine. Stop fussing over me."

"How can you be fine?" she countered. "You're acting like you haven't just lost your husband, not to mention Lucy."

The other woman shot Nadine a quelling look. "If she says she's fine, then she is."

"Stop talking about me as if I'm not here," Maeve huffed, rising regally to her feet. "I'm not a fragile hothouse flower."

Skye looked at Judy first, then the others. "Why don't you fetch her some lemonade?"

"I don't need a drink," she stated calmly. "But I would like for you all to return to your booths. We have money to raise for our charity. We want to exceed our amounts from last year."

The other woman hooked her arm through Nadine's and led her away.

Judy lingered, twisting her hands. "Please listen to the deputy."

"You may go, Judy."

Dismissed, Judy scurried out after the other women.

Skye studied Maeve's face, searching for signs she was truly in need of medical attention.

"I'm going upstairs. Will you accompany me?" Maeve asked. "I'd like to talk about Lucy."

She started for the rear stairs, reachable through a side exit door.

"What's upstairs?" Skye followed her.

"Mrs. Willoughby is certain there's a family heirloom up here. If I find it, she's agreed to donate a hefty sum to our charity."

The mercantile belonged to the Willoughby family. Bernice was the only one left, and she was too feeble to climb the stairs, much less pick through decades of belongings.

At the top, Skye surveyed the assortment of boxes, furniture and random items cluttering the massive space. Dusty light filtered in through the dirty windows spaced evenly apart. She followed the haphazard path behind Maeve. The dust tickled her nose, and she sneezed.

"What are you looking for exactly?"

"A music box." Her floral skirt flapped around her calves, and her sensible, thick-soled sandals squeaked on the slats. "Mrs. Willoughby claims it's inside her grandmother's dresser. The dresser is mahogany with a curved base, marble top and scrolled mirror. Shouldn't be too difficult to find."

They encountered several dressers that didn't fit the description. Finally, they found what they were looking for near a window overlooking the flower vendors. Maeve pulled out the middle drawer and uttered a triumphant sound.

"Here it is."

"Mrs. Willoughby will be pleased," Skye remarked, swiping a cobweb from her sleeve.

"Not to mention our charity will benefit."

Skye studied Maeve. "Have you thought about the plans for Virgil's funeral?"

Maeve's fingernails went white against the ornate box. "I don't want to talk about it."

The woman was in serious denial. Who could blame her? Skye knew from experience what it was like to suffer loss with an entire town watching. Everyone had different expectations about the proper way to grieve. Before she could think of something helpful to say, Maeve stated it was time to go.

More than happy to leave this stuffy, spider-filled place, Skye turned. There was a thump, and Maeve cried out.

Skye pivoted and rushed to help the older woman, who was on her knees and struggling to rise.

"I dropped the music box. Can you reach it?"

"Let me help you first."

"I'm okay. I just don't want anything to happen to that box."

Skye lowered herself onto one knee beside Maeve and reached between a broken TV set and a cabinet. There was a flurry of movement beside her, and she felt a sharp tug on her duty belt. The solid weight of her gun was no longer against her hip.

"Maeve?" Shifting, she lifted her head and stared up at her own service weapon.

"Get up."

The serene Southern belle Maeve Ackerman exemplified was gone. Her features were almost unrecognizable. Her mouth was a surly slash, her nostrils flared, her eyes sharp and cunning.

Shock shimmered through Skye as she slowly gained her footing. "What's going on, Maeve?"

"It's always the same," she griped. "'What are you doing, Maeve?'" she mimicked. "You all should ask what you're doing to make my life unbearable."

"No. Not you." Skye wrestled with disbelief. "Lucy was your daughter. Your own flesh and blood."

"Lucy was a disgrace. An embarrassment. If she'd obeyed me from the start, she would've been the biggest success story in Tulip's history. I would've had a daughter I could be proud of. But she was rebellious to the core. I blame her biological father for that."

The hateful words cut at Skye. How could any mother speak about her child like that? "Why kill her, though? She wasn't living in Tulip anymore."

"Simple. Eden."

Skye blinked. "She kept her a secret from you, and you were angry."

"Lucy was the ultimate failure. With Eden, I'll have a fresh start." Her gaze narrowed. "I didn't anticipate anyone in Tulip being the father. Nash's paternity put a wrench in my plans. Then you had to poke your nose where it doesn't belong. You and Nash have to be taken care of."

Skye's mind quailed at the knowledge of how much time this unhinged woman had already had with Eden. She and Nash had trusted her implicitly. *God, please, don't let this woman get access to Eden. Don't let evil win.*

"Was it you who shot at us on the ranch and at the bed-and-breakfast? And what about the graveyard? You were watching Eden that night."

"I can see you're surprised." She smirked. "My grandpa was a hunter. I was practically born with a gun in my hand. Babysitting Eden was the perfect cover. Virgil was home that night. I made up a fake emergency and had him stay with her. When I returned, I sent him to the store so you couldn't interview him."

"How did you maneuver me into that car trunk?"

"I'm stronger than I look." She scowled. "I couldn't manage Virgil on my own, though. I had to pay someone to bury him. He did a poor job of it."

"Who was it? Did you kill him, too?"

"Doesn't matter. And no, I didn't kill him."

"You won't get away with this."

"No one will suspect me. You didn't." Her gloating made Skye feel ill. "Everyone thinks it's either Zane or Bubba. Or both. Their history with Lucy played perfectly into my plans."

"Three witnesses can place you with me. We're surrounded by people right outside this building."

Maeve glanced around. "These historic buildings are important to our heritage, but sometimes they have hidden dangers. Did you know the floor back there is unstable? This building is unique. During the renovations, they removed the second floor to give the main space a better sense of grandeur. That means the distance between this floor and the ground is substantial. Unfortunately, you're unlikely to survive such a fall. If you do, you'll be like your poor little sister, Dove, unable to interact with the world. I'll be sure to speak at your funeral." She motioned with the gun, snagging a pillow from a box—presumably to use as a makeshift silencer. "Let's get moving, Deputy. I have flowers to sell."

Skye reluctantly wove through the mess toward the back wall, where there was a small clearing. If she reached for her phone, would Maeve pull the trigger? If she called out for help, would anyone hear her?

She stopped and turned, hoping to buy herself some time. "Why kill Virgil?"

Maeve rolled her eyes. "Virgil was yet another person who refused to heed my wishes. He was supposed to stay in town until the dust settled, but he kept flitting in and out and drawing suspicion. That was too close for comfort, so I took care of it."

She spoke nonchalantly about ending a human life. And not a random stranger. She'd killed her own husband and daughter.

"Eden is malleable," she said. "I can already see that she'll be bendable to my will."

Fury seethed in Skye's core. "You'll never get your hands on her."

One brow arched. "Won't I? Your death is going to look like an accident. I'm sure I can eventually arrange something for Nash, as well. Did you know freak accidents happen all the time on farms and ranches?"

Skye debated whether or not to risk a bullet.

Maeve's features hardened. "If you try anything, I'll make sure Nash's death is slow and agonizing. I know how to inflict pain. Lucy begged for mercy."

Skye's stomach heaved, and she pressed her hand to her mouth. Was this truly the end for her? The tragedy wasn't lost on her. She'd finally fallen in love.

The memory of Lucy's final moments made the decision easy. She couldn't risk Nash suffering that kind of pain.

God, please show me a way out of this.

"How did you overpower Virgil?"

"I made sure he had one too many drinks with dinner."

Maeve advanced on her, and Skye edged back. The floor groaned beneath her weight. There were uneven saw marks in the worn slats.

"Keep going," Maeve ordered.

Skye took another backward step. There was a shift and pop, and a portion of the slat beneath her right foot gave way. Arms outstretched, she careened sideways, barely managing to stay upright.

Seconds later, the board slammed into the floor far below.

Maeve smirked. "Hear that? Imagine what your bones are going to do upon impact."

Skye hadn't faced evil before. It was a chilling experience. She wished Lucy had been spared. Now it fell to Skye to spare Eden a life of nightmares.

She lunged. Maeve pulled the trigger.

Skye dived for cover, landing on the compromised slats. Her weight dislodged them, and she felt herself falling. A scream ripping out of her, she scrabbled for something to hold on to.

Nash couldn't find Skye. Dax, who'd sheepishly admitted to making up an excuse to attend the festival, said he'd last seen Skye a little more than half an hour ago. Nash searched around the food vendors, remembering all too well how she'd been taken from the rodeo. His chest felt tight, and the vise around his middle wasn't going to release until he set eyes on her.

He was approaching the flower section when he heard a high-pitched scream coming from inside the old mercantile. The people closest to the building stopped what they were doing and craned their necks, trying to find the source. Those farther away continued about their business.

Nash skirted the booth nearest the front doors.

Judy accosted him. "Did you hear that? Maeve and Skye are in there."

"Get help," he urged. Had the killer cornered the women?

"Skye?" he called out, darting through the cavernous space. "Maeve?"

"Help! Up here!"

Nash's vision adjusted to the low light, allowing him to see the woman hanging suspended far above the stage. He recognized Skye's uniform and shoes swinging in midair.

"Skye!" Racing toward her, he searched for something, anything, to fix this.

Seeing nothing, he made the decision to try to help her from above. "Hold on! I'm coming up there!"

He took the stairs two at a time. At the top, he barreled through the clutter, only to stop short when he saw Maeve holding a gun.

She stared at him with murder in her eyes. "Goodbye, Nash. Don't worry—I'll take good care of my granddaughter after you're gone."

Everything seemed to happen in slow motion. She pulled the trigger. He leaped to the floor, rolled out of the way, jumped to his feet and charged her.

She went down with an outraged grunt and a thump. The gun went flying and was eaten up by the debris.

Skye's hold on the single slat began to slip.

"Nash, I can't hold on," she gasped, her eyes stark.

He crawled over Maeve to get to Skye.

"No!" Skye warned. "It's not stable."

He scooted on his belly, hands outstretched, desperate to save her. He didn't care that Maeve was getting away. Saving this woman was all that mattered.

Beneath him, the weakened wood began to crack and split.

"Take my hand," he ordered.

"I don't think I can."

Nash inched closer, sweat rolling off him, prayers forming at breakneck pace.

I can't lose her, Lord. We need her, Eden and I both.

When he was within reach, he latched on to her wrist. "I've got you. Take my other hand."

She bit her lip.

"I'm not losing you today, Skye Saddler." Or any other day, if he had his way. "You can do this."

With his free hand, he held his fingers centimeters from hers. Determination stole over her face as she let go. Her body swung away, and she screamed. Nash seized her other wrist and heaved with all his might, pulling her halfway through the hole. The boards beneath him began to snap. His arms tightening around her, he rolled them away from the danger, knocking into boxes.

The wood bouncing against the stage below sounded like thunderclaps. Skye scrambled off him, grasped his arms and dragged him farther into the room.

After helping each other stand, he framed her face. "Are you okay?"

Her eyes were huge. "I'm not hurt. It was Maeve all along, Nash." Her voice broke. "You should've heard her talking about Lucy. No." She shook her head. "I'm glad you didn't."

It would take some time for the revelation to sink in. "We have to find her."

Holding hands, they batted their way back to the stairs. Outside, they found a confused Judy.

"Where's Maeve?" he demanded, unholstering his weapon and handing it to Skye. Nodding her thanks, she got on her radio and requested assistance.

"She was in a hurry." Judy pointed toward the fruit-and-vegetable section. "She almost knocked me down and didn't even apologize."

Together, Nash and Skye raced through the crowd. Skidding into the aisle where the jam contest was under-way, Skye pointed.

"Is that her? Sneaking behind that ancient truck?"

"Looks like her."

Pushing between the truck and the nearby canopy, they entered a deserted space lined with the backsides of tents. Maeve had almost reached the parking lot, where she no doubt had her getaway car ready.

Skye caught up to her and tackled her to the ground.

She handcuffed Maeve and read her her rights. Sheriff Hines and Chen jogged over. Hank approached at a more sedate pace.

"Saddler, what's the meaning of this?" Hines demanded.

Out of breath, Skye managed an explanation. "Maeve Ackerman is under arrest for the murders of Lucy and Virgil Ackerman and the attempted murders of Nash and myself."

Chen made a scoffing sound. "You expect me to believe it was her?"

Nash glared at the man. "You'll find her fingerprints on Skye's gun and the casing of the bullet she fired at me in the mercantile storage space."

"There will likely also be a handsaw somewhere in the debris," she added, "proving she deliberately compromised the floor before ordering me to stand on it."

By this time, curious onlookers had gathered in the parking lot behind the men. Some were already using their phones to take pictures and video.

"Get those people out of here!" Maeve shrieked. "If any of you puts this online, I'll sue!"

Sheriff Hines frowned at the woman lying prone on the ground. "You're in no position to make demands, Maeve." He ordered Chen and Hank to round up the saw and Skye's weapon. Looking over at Skye with obvious admiration, he said, "Good work, Saddler. I'll take it from here. You can help with crowd control."

Skye glanced at Nash as if she couldn't quite believe it was over. The case was resolved. Lucy and Virgil would get justice. No more looking over their shoulders or worrying about the next assault.

Chen stormed past them, mumbling under his breath. Hank paused and patted Skye's arm, congratulating her on a job well done. Skye moved into the parking lot to try to control the gathering crowd. Nash followed, needing to be near her, hoping she didn't mind. Was she ready to kick him out of her life now that the case was solved?

After Sheriff Hines had Maeve in his cruiser, the crowd began to disperse. Nash couldn't wait a second longer.

"I need to talk to you."

"What is it?"

"Not here." Heart hammering in his chest, he took her hand and drew her away from the festival site and over to the adjacent pond. Up ahead, there was a gazebo beneath a massive oak tree. Its branches granted them privacy.

"If you're bringing me out here to talk about how

things are going to be now that the case is over, I'd like to ask that I still be allowed to spend time with Eden."

His lungs deflated. "Of course. I want you to spend time with her. She loves you."

Her eyes watered. "I love her, too. Thank you, Nash."

He licked his suddenly dry lips. If she cared for him, she would've said so, right? Maybe he should end it here. Save himself the heartache and humiliation.

"No need to thank me. I want what's best for her," he said slowly. Her smile seemed strained, her eyes sad. "Actually, I owe you a heap of gratitude. You put your all into protecting us."

"I wouldn't change a thing."

"Me, either." *Except maybe that disastrous proposal.*

"Is there anything else you'd like to say?" she prompted.

Yes. Tons more. But his feelings and wishes were too big to voice.

"I, uh, will be happy to help you move to Honoria's."

The light in her eyes dimmed. "I don't need help. I don't have that much to move."

He gritted his teeth. Why was this so difficult?

She started backing away. "I'm going to the station. They'll need my statement. I have a report to file. You'll be asked to come in and give your statement, too."

He fisted his hands.

"I'll see you around, cowboy." She presented him with her back and started for the path.

His heart did a rebellious dance. *Are you really going to let her go without a fight?*

"Skye, wait." He dashed in front of her and rested his hands on her shoulders. "I do have more to say. This time with you has changed everything. Before you moved to the ranch, I still saw you as that sassy, in-your-face young girl who disapproved of everything I said and did. I don't know why I didn't make the effort to get to know you once I moved home. I guess I figured your opinion of me hadn't changed, so why try?"

A shadow passed over her eyes and she opened her mouth to speak. He slid his hands down her arms and lightly grasped her hands.

"Let me get this out, please, before I lose my nerve. It didn't take long for me to realize I never knew the true you. I was surprised by how kind and gentle you were with Eden. You didn't judge me for my mistakes, and you encouraged me in what has been the most difficult season of my life. You brought joy to a little girl who'd lost her mom and to me, a clueless cowboy who didn't know the first thing about being a father."

He took a deep, shuddering breath. "I thought a marriage of convenience was what I wanted. Then we kissed, and I knew I couldn't be in a relationship with you and keep my heart boxed in. Skye, please don't walk out of my life. I couldn't bear it." He sucked in another fortifying breath. "I love you."

Joy burst across her face. Slipping her hands free, she framed his face and kissed him soundly.

"I love you, Nash Wilder. I was wrong about you back then, and I was wrong about the adult you, too. I find it hard to believe we've lived in the same town and never knew how wonderful we could be together. We could've missed out on this."

He pressed a gentle kiss to her lips, breathing in her scent and closeness. "God took a terrible situation and brought something good from it."

She nodded soberly. "I'm learning He uses all sorts of things to grow our faith. I'm grateful He's patient with us and never gives up. I've also learned I can't go through life alone. He's taught me the importance of community."

"I'm ready to make new memories together in Tulip. Aren't you?"

"Starting with more kisses," she teased, bringing her face close again.

"There will never be enough of those," he laughed.

He was the most blessed cowboy in Mississippi.

EPILOGUE

"Can I open my eyes?"

"Not yet."

Nash had his arm around Skye as he led her through the house. A door opened, and the scent of rain-washed grass and soft earth wafted over her.

"Watch your step."

He guided her through the opening. Birdsong and the sun on her face told her they were on the patio, one of their favorite spaces to spend time together. In the five months since Maeve's arrest, Skye had spent more time at the ranch than in the camper she'd bought and parked at Honoria's. Nash liked to grill, and Skye liked to eat. It was a winning combination. As the evenings lost the searing heat of late summer, they'd taken to huddling on the couch before the fire and helping Eden roast marshmallows.

Eden was with Honoria tonight. Nash had planned a surprise for Skye's birthday. True to character, he'd kept that surprise a secret, despite her wheedling. She'd taken a day off, and he'd handed the ranch operations to Hardy. Nash had taken her to Biloxi, where they'd eaten their fill of fresh seafood, browsed waterfront shops and enjoyed a leisurely boat ride. It seemed the surprises weren't over.

He guided her around the furniture. "You can open them now."

The patio table had been draped with a white cloth, barely visible beneath a spread worthy of the finest Biloxi hotel. Casting a smile at Nash, who was watching her closely, his blue eyes dancing in the sunset, she ventured closer.

"This is basically a waffle buffet." She laughed, swiping a dollop of whipped cream and savoring the pleasant almond flavor.

The outer rim was comprised of shiny platters piled with waffles. Some were studded with berries, some with nuts, others with sausage, bacon and cheese. There were also several toppings to choose from.

Unable to resist, she selected a savory waffle and sampled it. Groaning, she handed it to him to try. "Who made these? I need the recipe."

He swallowed a bite and shook his head. "They're not as good as yours."

"This is wonderful, Nash."

"Happy birthday, darlin'." He leaned over and kissed her cheek in the sensitive spot near her ear. She shifted her face and kissed him square on the mouth.

"This is the best birthday. Thank you for making it special."

He handed her a plate. "Eat up. There's more to come."

"More surprises?" She glanced at the bounty before her. "What can possibly top this?"

His low, husky laugh wrapped around her, and she was tempted to pinch herself. These months with Nash had felt like a wonderful, impossible dream. The more she got to know him, the more she loved about him. Beneath the rough-and-tumble exterior beat a sensitive heart. He was attentive to her needs and thoughtful to boot. Most importantly, he'd helped her grow closer to the Lord.

Grinning, he shook his head. "You won't get a word out of me."

They ate together on the couch and soaked in the autumn landscape. Her life was fuller now than it had been before. God had created something beautiful out of the sadness. The town was still coming to terms with the revelation that their stalwart do-gooder had deceived everyone.

During the investigation, troubling facts had come to light about Maeve's past. She'd been abused by her father as a child, which had led to an obsessive need to control everything and everyone around her. They'd looked into her first husband's death and, after exhuming his body, had discovered she'd poisoned him. Maeve's reason? He'd refused to take a job she'd wanted for him. Virgil's frequent absences during their long marriage had spared him until he'd bucked her wishes during the investigation.

They'd learned the man who'd buried Virgil had been in and out of jail for petty crimes. He'd stayed in Tulip even after Maeve's arrest and, when questioned, readily admitted his role.

To avoid the publicity of a trial, Maeve had pleaded guilty and would spend the rest of her life in prison. It wouldn't bring back Lucy, but justice had been served.

"What are you thinking about?"

She looked up to find Nash's plate cleared. He was sipping orange juice, his loving gaze on her.

Placing her plate on the coffee table, she leaned into his side. He welcomed her, hugging her close and dropping a kiss on her head.

"Do you think Lucy would approve of us?"

He lazily rubbed her arm. "The father of her child and her best friend together? I think she'd be shocked, like a lot of people in Tulip, but happy for all three of us."

She smiled. It had taken people a while to get used to the idea. Grace had decided not to try. She'd handed in her resignation and left the area.

"Can I have my next surprise now?"

Chuckling, he stood, took her hands and hauled her up. "It's out front."

Skye hadn't seen anything unusual when they'd returned from Biloxi. Anticipation danced along her spine. So far, Nash was proving he had mad birthday skills.

They walked around the side of the house to the driveway.

Her jaw dropped. "That's for me?"

She gawked at the blue food truck. *The Skye's the Limit* was painted in bold font on the side, with drool-worthy photos of thick golden waffles underneath.

"I can return it if you decide it's not for you," Nash said quickly. "You haven't been happy with your job for some time, and your waffle stand has been a huge hit at the farmers' markets this summer. I thought, why not make it full-time?"

Skye's eyes filled with tears and she pressed her hand to her mouth.

His shoulder brushed hers. "You don't like it. It's fine, darlin'."

"No, I love it," she murmured, trying to wrangle her emotions. "No one has ever done anything this grand for me before. Your belief in me is overwhelming."

Facing her, he cupped her shoulders. "I believe you can do anything, Skye Saddler, with God's help, of course." His gaze was intense. "There's one more thing. Hardy? We're ready."

Skye turned to see Hardy beside the fence. He lowered Eden to the ground, and she ran to them, a sweetheart in a bright pink dress. Hardy waved and sauntered off.

Eden's sweet face was alight. "'Kye! 'Kye!" She handed her a gift bag and pointed to the truck. "Big truck!"

Skye laughed. Eden had grown more animated and energetic over the summer, and she'd wormed her way even deeper into Skye's heart.

While Eden ogled the truck, Nash instructed Skye to open the gift. Her heart soared when she saw the tiny velvet box. Inside, a sparkling diamond ring was nestled in the folds. She gasped. Looking up, she found Nash down on one knee, his blue eyes full of love.

"I love you, Skye, and I want nothing more than to spend the rest of my life with you. Will you be my wife?"

"Yes!" She threw her arms around his neck and showered him with kisses.

Eden danced around them, parroting her. "Yes! Yes! Yes!"

The rumble of a large moving truck pulling up the drive drowned out their laughter. Skye cocked her head. "Another surprise, Nash?"

"Not of my doing." He stood, his forehead wrinkling. "Is that Remi?"

The truck rumbled to a stop, and Remi leaped to the ground, arms thrown wide. "Surprise!"

Eden ran up to Remi, who scooped her into her arms. "How's my favorite cowgirl?" As she walked over with Eden in her arms, she gawked at the food truck. "What's this?"

"I'm hanging up my uniform and putting on an apron," Skye told her. "That's not the best news." Skye held up her left hand and wiggled her fingers.

"You're engaged?" Squealing, Remi wrapped her free arm around Skye. "I'm getting a sister!"

Skye's happiness was bittersweet. "I wish Dove could celebrate with us."

Nash wrapped his arm around her, his smile encompassing them. "Why don't we go see her right now? We can tell her the news."

Skye nodded in agreement. "She'll like that."

God had gifted her a family, right here in her hometown.

* * * * *

If you enjoyed this story, look for these other books by Karen Kirst:

Mountain Murder Investigation
Smoky Mountain Ambush

Dear Reader,

God often brings good out of tough situations. Skye thought He'd abandoned her, but she couldn't have been more wrong. Whenever you're suffering hardships, turn to Him. He will welcome you with open arms.

I hope you've enjoyed this first book in Tulip, Mississippi. I certainly enjoyed getting to know these new characters and look forward to revisiting them in Remi's story. This is my third suspense series. If you'd like to learn about the others, which feature military heroes and mounted police, please visit my website, www.karenkirst.com. You can sign up for my newsletter there. I'm also active on Facebook.

God Bless,
Karen Kirst

HARLEQUIN
PLUS

Try the best multimedia subscription service for romance readers like you!

Read, Watch and Play.

Experience the easiest way to get the romance content you crave.

Start your **FREE TRIAL** at
www.harlequinplus.com/freetrial.